T0099701

DOTS

John Patch

Order this book online at www.trafford.com
or email orders@trafford.com

Most Trafford titles are also available at major online book retailers.

© Copyright 2010 John Patch.
All rights reserved. No part of this publication may be reproduced, stored
in a retrieval system, or transmitted, in any form or by any means, electronic,
mechanical, photocopying, recording, or otherwise, without
the written prior permission of the author.

The characters and events in this book are fictitious. Any similarity to real
persons, living or dead, is coincidental and not intended by the author.

Printed in the United States of America.

ISBN: 978-1-4269-4587-8 (sc)
ISBN: 978-1-4269-4670-7 (e)

*Our mission is to efficiently provide the world's finest, most comprehensive
book publishing service, enabling every author to experience success.
To find out how to publish your book, your way, and have it available
worldwide, visit us online at www.trafford.com*

Trafford rev. 11/03/2010

 www.trafford.com

North America & international
toll-free: 1 888 232 4444 (USA & Canada)
phone: 250 383 6864 ♦ fax: 812 355 4082

CHAPTER 1

May 23, 1978

Mary Robbins asked herself again what she was doing there. She was 24 years old. At 5'6" and 124 pounds, she was an attractive brown-haired woman who very nicely filled out the bikini she was wearing.

She was nearing the close of her third year of teaching English at Burlington High School. Today was a day off for her. This was exam week and she had no exams scheduled to give until tomorrow.

Mary was with an 18-year-old senior whom she had been tutoring for the past two school years. They were out on Lake Champlain in his family's boat, anchored in a secluded cove off from the southwestern tip of the island.

It is located just around the corner and out of view from Burlington Harbor, and Shelburne Point. The closest clear line of sight into the cove was from the New York shoreline more than seven miles to the west. This early in the boating season there was virtually no traffic on the lake on a Thursday afternoon.

Mary had been very careful to cover her tracks. She had walked from her home in the small housing development adjacent to Shelburne Shipyard near the tip of Shelburne Point.

She had not drawn undue attention, because she took this same walk almost every day that she was at home. The path to the end of the point ran for a ways parallel to the marina at Shelburne Shipyard.

When she reached the point on the path where it was closest to the back of the marina, she had paused and looked around carefully. She waited until no one was in sight before cutting off the path.

Mary slipped into the marina yard and worked her way among the many boats still in their cradles. She went down to the dock where a 25-foot yellow and white Donzi speedboat was tied up. She quickly climbed aboard and hid in the small unlocked cuddy cabin.

Her student came aboard a few minutes later. He told the dock boy who had been standing over at the gas dock that he was going to perform the start of season "sea trials" with the boat. No one else knew Mary was on board. No one else knew about their affair.

Last February he had become her lover. Mary had been tutoring him since the start of his junior year. In February, he had given her a Valentine card and an expensive watch as a gift. She had given him a thank you kiss that instantly became more. She had been starved for attention. He was a horny eighteen-year-old senior and the results were predictable.

They left the shipyard marina and rounded Shelburne Point before Mary came out of the cuddy cabin and took off her shorts and tee shirt.

After a quick boat ride down past the Shelburne Farms Brick House a few miles south of the point, they turned around and made their way back up to the cove to spend the afternoon together.

They opened a couple of beers and started to talk. This was the first time that they had been together outside of the scheduled times that Mary had been tutoring him at his parent's home.

They were both a little nervous about the possibility of being discovered. After a half hour and a few more beers they became more relaxed and started to kiss. It did not take too long for their swimsuits to come off.

After they had made love, still naked and slightly buzzed from the beer she had consumed, Mary dove into the frigid 60-degree water from the stern of the boat. The unseen large rock was 3 ½ feet below the surface of the lake.

When her head slammed into it, her skull had broken, sending a large sharp shard deep into her brain. She had died instantly. The red of her blood mixing with the lake water floated to the surface before her body did.

Her young lover seeing the bloody water screamed to her "are you alright?" When she didn't respond he jumped in and franticly pulled her lifeless body back into the stern of the boat and attempted to revive her.

After several minutes, he accepted the futility of his efforts. He stopped and stared at her body searching his mind trying to decide what he should do next.

Not wanting to embarrass his family by having the affair discovered and not knowing what else to do, he pulled Mary's bikini, shorts, tee shirt, and shoes back onto her body in the back of the boat.

Then, he took two oversized beach towels out of the cuddy cabin and wrapped those around her. Finally, he pulled up the anchor and drove out of the cove into the broad lake.

Cutting the motor after reaching a spot located directly west of the island, he took the anchor and rode and wrapped her shrouded body securely with them. He pulled her over the stern and then rolled her onto the swim platform.

Finally, he used a small manual bilge pump to flush the bloody carpet with lake water where her body had lain. He then started the motor again and steered the boat to a spot south of the island where the depth finder showed 340 feet of water under the boat.

He cut the motor again and rolled Mary's body off the swim platform. He immediately restarted the boat and headed back to Shelburne Shipyard and his slip. Quickly securing the dock lines and fenders, he went to his car and drove home. The secret was safe.

Since that day, he seldom went near the boat again, never without another family member along.

CHAPTER 2

Mary Collins had met her future husband, Gary Robbins during November of her sophomore year attending the University of Vermont. She was from a small town in Pennsylvania and he was a Burlington native. She had gone downtown to a popular local bar called Hannibal's with several of her girl friends.

Gary and some of his friends were there celebrating a UVM hockey win over Harvard. The Robbins family were big supporters of the hockey program. The new scoreboard hanging in Gutterson Arena had been a gift from them.

Mary was impressed by his gregarious nature. Mary's great looks and model-like body impressed Gary. They ended up at his apartment.

Gary's father owned several auto parts stores in the Burlington area, which he would take over when his dad retired. In the meantime, he managed the warehouse in Essex Junction.

Mary moved into his apartment at the start of her junior year. Her parents were less than thrilled about Mary living with a man to whom she was not married. They had urged her to take things slowly.

Gary had asked Mary to marry him during semester break her senior year. She accepted. They had a large ceremony and elaborate reception at the Marble Island Resort following her graduation in early June.

After the honeymoon, they moved into a colonial style house located in a desirable development on Shelburne Point. Gary's parents had given it to them as a wedding present. A few months later everything in their marriage changed.

Gary went out partying with the boys almost every night right after work. When he stumbled drunkenly into their bedroom in the early morning hours he smelled of expensive booze and cheap women.

Mary held her tongue as long as she could. She hoped that Gary would realize how much she loved him and would change his behavior.

Shortly after their first anniversary, she could stand it no longer. She attempted to discuss her feelings with him one night when he came home unusually early and almost sober.

"Gary, you don't realize how much you are hurting our marriage because of your behavior. If you can't change your habits and show respect for our marriage then I will be forced to leave you. I love you and want to make this work. Please promise me that you'll stop whoring around."

Gary had responded by beating the hell out of her. "If you ever try to leave I will ruin your life". She believed him. She knew that she would have to plan very carefully and secretly if she decided to escape.

Teaching then became Mary's safe haven. She loved the respect it gave her from the community and the kids she taught. She started to do tutoring after school.

This gave her an excuse to not have to go right home each day, and she could put away part of the money to help her leave him.

They became enemies living in the same house. Mary could not wait for her opportunity to flee her disastrous marriage.

After her disappearance, Gary Robbins was the prime suspect. The case was unofficially closed 10 years later after Mary was pronounced dead by the court at her family's request.

CHAPTER 3

May 2005

Jack Johnson knew that he needed to pay his respects, but it did not make it any easier to be here. Dealing with death had never come easily to him. He knew that his late father Newell would have wanted the family represented and Jack felt it to be his responsibility to see it done.

He was standing in the slowly moving receiving line at Preston's Funeral Home. Preston's was a fourth generation family run business located in downtown Burlington a few blocks off from Church Street's downtown shopping district in the heart of the city.

The mortuary was a small painted brick building with a wooden ell built off the north end of the original structure. It had low ceilings and outdated dark paneling on the walls.

The carpet was old and there was a faint musty odor in the air. The parking lot was small, but adequate for most of the wakes and services that were held there.

The families that used Preston's Funeral Home instead of one of the larger, newer mortician services available were almost exclusively from the "old north end" of Burlington.

They chose it because of its history with their families. Many of the bodies prepared and displayed there were those of children and grandchildren of past customers.

The Preston family had served the needs of the families from Burlington's old north end for over 100 years and in return, the majority of the old north end families supported the Preston family business.

Bennie Richards had grown up in Burlington's old north end on Lakeview Terrace. The neighborhood was transitioning now.

Until the 1990's it was run down single family and multi-family houses with a view of old fuel storage tanks. They had been used to store gasoline and heating oil until the 1980's, when the oil companies had ceased shipping it from New York by barge.

There were dilapidated waterfront warehouses that had been abandoned for many years. The unused Moran Generating Plant also oversaw the scene. It was a giant coal burning electric plant that had supplied much of Burlington's electricity needs before the advent of nuclear power and had been shut down in the 1970's.

It had always been a working class neighborhood. Families had been living in the same houses and apartments for generations.

Several of the adjoining neighborhoods had been bulldozed in the early 1960's as part of the urban renewal project that was slowly transforming Burlington's downtown back into a viable city center.

The Richards' house had been built in the late 1890's or early 1900's as workers housing for the mills. His parents had bought it using his father's GI bill following his army service during the Korean conflict in the early 1950's.

There were three apartments in the building, two in the "big house" close to the street. The third had been converted from an old adjoining shed and garage.

It was out behind the big house in the back yard, and had lake views. As a child, Bennie lived in the back unit with his parents. The rent from the front apartments had helped with the mortgage payments during lean times.

Bennie's father had worked at a service station located at the foot of Main Street. The Richards couldn't afford a car, so he walked to and from work each day. His place of employment was just five blocks from the house.

His mother took a job at Marble Island after Bennie started first grade. They could finally afford an old second hand sedan.

A few years later, his dad opened his own service station. It was located on the corners of South Winooski Avenue and Main Street. It was just up the hill from where he had been working since he had gotten out of the service.

Bennie had been one of those kids in school that had always been on the fringe of the action, trying to become a player with the in crowd.

He wanted to belong, but because he came from the old north end and his family was blue collar he could never gain acceptance from the group of kids that he so much wanted to join.

Even after Bennie had finished high school almost thirty years ago, he had never stopped trying to belong to the in crowd.

Three days ago, he had died in a single car accident. He left behind his mother, his widow and two teenage kids. They were all still living in the rear apartment on Lakeview Terrace.

Bennie's wake was sparsely attended. A few of his friends, some customers from the neighborhood mini mart he had operated with his mom, a few business acquaintances, his family, Jack, and lastly a surprise appearance by the mayor of Burlington, Louis O'Brien IV.

Jack wondered why the recently elected Mayor was attending the wake. Most of the small group of people that was there were Bennie's contemporaries. There was no way Louis IV fit in with that group.

Jack went through the line with the others, when he got to Bennie's mother he extended his condolences and she asked him to accompany her outside for a smoke.

Jack had first met Jean Richards when his father had moved the Johnson family to Burlington from Rutland in October 1966. She had been the short order cook and kitchen manager at the Marble Island Hotel and Resort. Jack, a freshman in high school, was a part-time dishwasher and bus boy.

The Marble Island Resort was not really on Marble Island, but at the end of the peninsula that lead to it.

The island itself is a very small piece of real estate that acted as a natural breakwater for the marina docks from strong north winds. The main structure was an old white two-story building that had started life a large farmhouse.

Over the past fifty years it had been added to with a north and south wing, as well as a large meeting facility on the east side of the building overlooking the marina and docks.

There was also an Olympic size swimming pool, three clay tennis courts, and a nine hole golf course complete with pro shop.

Malletts Bay was on Lake Champlain. Sometimes referred to as the sixth great lake, Champlain is the largest natural freshwater lake located entirely in the United States. 116 miles long and 12 miles wide at its widest point, it delineated most of the Vermont/New York border.

Its historical significance dated back almost 400 years to when Samuel D'Champlain had explored and claimed it for the French Crown.

It was then won first by the British during the French and Indian War, and then the American Colonists during the Revolutionary War.

Many historians have pronounced it as the location of the turning point of the Revolution. It also played an instrumental part in the British defeat in the War of 1812.

A restored fort still stands in Ticonderoga, New York. Thousands of tourists visit it each summer. The Lake Champlain Chamber of Commerce, representing the greater

Burlington Vermont area, advertises Lake Champlain as the west coast of New England.

Jack's father, Newell Johnson, had been hired to manage hotel and restaurant at the resort in 1966 by Charles O'Brien. It was an O'Brien family owned resort hotel and summer place that they had acquired during the depression.

Newell Johnson had thought the world of Jean Richards. She was dependable, conscientious, and acted like a surrogate mother to the young restaurant employees.

Jack's opinion and his fathers had concurred. Jean had always treated him with respect.

Working for his father had been rough duty. Newell demanded that Jack do more work for less money than the others did, because he was his son. Most of the dining room and kitchen staff had treated Jack like a leper because his dad was the manager.

Jean Richards had always treated him as she had everyone else. From her perspective, as long as Jack carried his weight he was as good as anyone who worked there.

When they got outside, Jean started the conversation.

"In my heart I know that Bennie's accident was no accident. He was going on his weekly run to pick up cigarette inventory for the mini mart. You could set the clock by Bennie's trip each Monday morning to the cigarette wholesaler's warehouse. He would leave the house at 6:00 A.M. make the drive to the warehouse in St. Albans and be at the mini mart by 8:30 A.M. He always went to Starbucks on Shelburne Road and filled his coffee cup, got on Interstate 89 and drove He wouldn't have fallen asleep."

Jack knew from the newspaper story that Bennie supposedly had done just that while at the wheel, and driven off interstate 89 at the Winooski River Bridge while traveling northbound. A state trooper setting up radar at 6:40 A.M. noticed tracks in the medium and investigated.

The trooper had followed the tracks and spotted Bennie's van laying upside down in the river 45 feet below. He had died on impact with the river bottom of massive head and neck injuries according to the article.

Jack asked "Jean what does your heart tell you happened?"

"Bennie had been excited lately. He told me that he had some inside information about something that was very precious to somebody who was important. He said he was going to sell it to him. The fee he would receive in exchange for his information would set him up financially. I'm certain that he was killed to prevent him from revealing the information."

"Could Bennie's wife Terry could shed any light on things?"

"Bennie confided very little in Terry. He told her nothing about it as it was not a sure thing yet and he was afraid that she would brag about their pending windfall to everyone that she knew. She isn't the sharpest knife in the drawer, and has never been able to keep a confidence."

Jack thought for a few minutes. "Jean I'll take a closer look at things and stop by the store to update you in a few days."

CHAPTER 4

When he left the wake, Jack started to think back to 39 years before. He had started at Burlington High School partway through his freshman year in 1966 when his family had moved to Burlington from Rutland Vermont, 70 miles to the south.

Jack never had time to join in the after school social scene because of his job at Marble Island. His parents had six kids, his mom did not work outside of the home and his father was not overpaid.

Not having to pay for Jack's clothes, books, or lunches took off at least a little of the strain. Besides, Jack liked being responsible for himself.

Because his parents could not afford to pay for his college, and Jack was not sufficiently motivated to do it on his own, when he graduated from high school in 1970, he had joined the Navy. It seemed a much better choice than wading through the rice paddies of Vietnam.

After four years as an MP on shore patrol, he came back to Burlington. While he had been away in the service, his high school sweetheart had married another man.

Jack joined the Burlington Police force as a patrol officer. A very short time later, he met and married a waitress/college student, Sally Williams, who had been working for his father at Marble Island.

He had spent the next 26 years as a Burlington cop. The first four were in uniform and the last twenty-two as detective.

Jack loved working with people. He found that working on crime puzzles was enjoyable and challenging. He also happened to be very good at it. Being a detective let him do two things that he truly enjoyed, while being paid for doing them.

When Jack had been working as a detective, Bennie Richards became a good source of information for him. The mini-mart Bennie operated with his mother had been converted from his father's old gas station. Bennie had hated pumping gas and changing tires. He had always wanted a clean job.

When his dad had died of a heart attack in 1980 at the age of 50, Bennie talked his mother into using the life insurance money to make the conversion into a mini mart with a deli.

Jean's ability to run the deli was what kept the business going. The large grocery stores sold goods for much less than Bennie could, so he specialized in beer and wine, liquor, cigarettes, magazines and other convenience items.

The mini-mart was located in downtown Burlington on the edge of the hill section. Bennie was a great eavesdropper.

When Jack needed to know about any questionable activities in the neighborhood, Bennie Richards was a fountain of knowledge.

He knew most of the wealthy homeowners and the working class tenants, the kids who hung out on Church Street, the downtown workers who came to the deli to pick up lunch, the college students, and the homeless population that lived down the hill on the waterfront in the old warehouses and in train cars.

He could tell which people belonged in the neighborhood and who did not fit. It was in his nature to share his insights if someone was of a mind to ask. Several times Jack had broken cases based on information Bennie had provided him.

In 1996, Bennie had approached Jack and asked to use his name as a reference with the State Liquor Control Board, so he could expand his business by selling hard liquor, Jack was happy to oblige.

CHAPTER 5

Louis O'Brien I had emigrated from Ireland in 1884 and found work as a machinist in the Burlington woolen mills. He was a hard worker and in a few years through his strong work ethic advanced to the position of shop foreman.

He saved a large portion of his pay and brought over his family from Ireland one by one. Louis found them work in the mills. The O'Brien clan pooled their resources and started purchasing rundown apartment houses in the old north end of Burlington. Over time, they became the biggest landlords in town.

The housing that the O'Brien family bought was all in poor shape. Most of their tenants could barely pay the rent. City officials decried the decrepit conditions that brought about numerous disease outbreaks.

There were occasional fatalities from fires caused by bad wiring, leaky gas lines, and/or inadequate heating systems.

However, the demand for housing far outweighed the supply, so little had been done to improve conditions.

Money bought the O'Brien family credibility. Louis's position as landlord to so many people bought political power.

Twelve years after emigrating from Ireland, Louis I won the first election campaign that he had ever entered. He became the mayor of Burlington Vermont.

His relatives and friends were given employment on the city payroll, and thus they became the center of the evolution of Burlington's development for the next two generations.

Money also gained the O'Brien's enemies. Burlington's elite shunned them as shanty Irish trash. It took more than money to belong to Burlington society. It took breeding to belong.

At the turn of the century, most of Burlington's old family's situations had gone into decline. Family fortunes had been made in woolen milling, quarrying marble, granite, and various ores, in turning logs into lumber, and shipping it from Lake Champlain, through the Champlain Canal to New York City and the world.

The advance of the Railroads combined with the increasing scarcity of easy mining opportunities, and the demise of shipping on inland waterways resulted in Burlington, once one of the largest ports in the inland United States, to become just another town in Vermont. Railroad tracks after all could run almost anywhere.

With the decline of their fortunes, the old families became jealous of anyone who was successful where they were not.

The immigrants should work for them in the mills, not try to better themselves.

Louis II had been groomed to carry on and expand the family dynasty. He graduated from The University of Vermont and went on to attend the Harvard Law School.

Upon completion of his education, he returned to Burlington and set up practice. His marriage to Marie Lawrence gained the O'Brien's their long sought social acceptance.

Marie's father had founded the Vermont Railroad. Unlike most of his contemporaries, James Lawrence had seen the changes coming. He had sold his interest in the Lake Champlain Steamship Company in the 1880's and used the proceeds to start the rail system.

At the turn of the 20th century, he controlled the entire western half of Vermont's rail lines from Bennington to Burlington. He was one of a very few from the hectic post civil war prosperity years to transition successfully to the twentieth century with his fortunes growing.

When Louis I retired from politics in the 1930's Louis II ran for and became mayor.

It was not from the political prominence, but from continuing and expanding other family business activities that he advanced the family fortunes.

The United States Cavalry had stationed an entire division at Fort Ethan Allen, just outside of Burlington in Colchester in the early 1900's. It was a large part of the Burlington area's economy throughout the depression era.

During prohibition, Louis II discovered that an astute businessman with inside knowledge of and influence over law enforcement activities could supply the troops with illegal refreshment and female companionship.

He could also curtail the efforts of his competition, using his father's mayoral influence over the police to attack and close down their enterprises. That, according to local folklore is precisely what the O'Brien family did, increasing their wealth substantially.

Louis II was smart about it. He kept himself distanced from the visible operations, and started giving to the city. The O'Brien wing of the library had been dedicated during that time, the first of several family memorials that exist today.

Louis II had loved to play poker. The Tuesday night games that he attended were held at Marble Island hosted by Charlie Flanagan who shared Louis II's love of gambling.

Charlie had built the place on the family farm when he returned from France where he had fought in World War I.

He figured that rich families from New York City and Boston would indulge in lengthy summer vacations. With the railroad running close by and Lake Champlain surrounding it, Marble Island should be a natural spot for them to escape to.

He was right. His lakefront hotel/spa was an instant success. The depression had hurt business, so the hotel was becoming run down.

One night when Charlie and Louis II were playing with the others in their regular game, Charlie had a particularly bad run of luck. Several times, he was bluffed into folding when he would have won.

Finally, he thought that he held a winning hand with a pair of tens and a pair of jacks. He was out of money. Certain that his hand was unbeatable Charlie bet the hotel. Louis II beat him with three lowly fives. He became the owner of the Marble Island Hotel as well as the surrounding farmland.

Not every business acquired during Louis II's reign was an illegal venture or won in a poker game. The depression brought about the collapse of many of Burlington's enterprises. The O'Brien family also acquired several legitimate businesses at very favorable prices due to the depression.

They had purchased a Buick dealership, the largest department store in the city, and a fledgling AM radio station, among others. All would prove to be profitable investments.

Louis III had been unable to continue with the family tradition successfully. Like his father, he had graduated from UVM and went off to Harvard to study the law. Then along came World War II.

He left law school and enlisted in the Army Air Corps serving as a bomber pilot. In 1943, his plane had been shot down over enemy territory.

He spent 1½ years as a prisoner of war in Germany before the war ended. His incarceration by the Germans had broken him both physically and mentally.

Louis III did have one grand idea for a business venture. He had bought Juniper Island, located at the gateway to Burlington Harbor on Lake Champlain, at a government auction of surplus property.

His grand plan was that because it was not a part of any municipality in Vermont and there were no restrictions on its use, he could develop it as a casino.

The only development on the island when Louis III acquired it had been a lighthouse and caretakers cottage. The Coast Guard had decommissioned the lighthouse at the close of the war.

He had a World War II surplus Jeep ferried to the island so that he could drive around. A bulldozer was also ferried across and was used to knock down the lighthouse and caretakers cottage. Louis III had the bulldozer clear a large flat area for an airstrip.

That is as far as he got on his grand scheme before the Vermont Supreme Court ruled that Juniper Island was part of Burlington and subject to their laws and regulations as well as their property taxes.

The project was abandoned. This was the last straw for his fragile mental state. Louis III would rarely visit the island again.

It was at that point that his younger brothers Charles and Frank stepped in and took over care of the family business interests. Louis III was an extremely well educated drunk.

His affable personality allowed his brothers to place him in the family owned Buick dealership. They put a strong but unseen manager behind the scenes to oversee the successful management of the business, and to keep Louis III out of serious trouble. Most of the embarrassing situations that arose with Louis III after that were swept under the rug.

John Patch

The most memorable that became public knowledge was when he and a female office worker from the dealership were found running down Church Street wearing only their birthday suits early one Sunday morning after the bars had closed down.

After that, his brothers sent him to a clinic to dry out, and kept him on a very short leash when he returned.

CHAPTER 6

Louis O'Brien IV had been the leader of the in crowd in high school. In many ways, his future had been decided for him even before he was born.

His family had now been a part of Burlington's elite for the past seventy-five years. As oldest male of his generation and namesake of the patriarch, he was in line to inherit the family throne.

After graduation from high school, Louis IV followed the course set by his grandfather and father. He went to UVM and upon graduation, he moved on to Harvard Law.

After earning his law degree and passing the bar exam on his first attempt, he joined the family's law firm, headed by his Uncle Frank. Louis IV specialized in corporate and environmental law. He worked hard and quickly become one of the most knowledgeable attorneys in Vermont about Act 250.

Act 250 is a land use master plan passed in the 1970's. The original premise of it was …to regulate and control the utilization and usages of lands and the environment to insure that, hereafter, the only usages which will be permitted are not unduly detrimental to the environment, will promote the general welfare through orderly growth and development and are suitable to the demands and needs of the people of this state

…Anyone may attend hearings, but only persons with party status may present evidence. Whether a person receives party status depends on such things as whether the individual's land borders the project's land, or whether the person is directly affected by the project, or whether his knowledge will significantly help the District Commission with its decision…

Over the years since Act 250's inception, developers, as well as many environmental groups had learned to use and misuse the law to their advantage.

This made building or developing any property extremely expensive and time consuming. Something that was previously as simple as a farmer subdividing his property to sell off a few building lots had become extremely difficult for landowners.

Obtaining the necessary permits required for drawing water out of a mountain stream or pond to make snow, or developing a new industrial park or suburban shopping mall had turned into a multimillion-dollar expense because of the red tape involved.

The complexity of the process sired a new type of attorney. Louis IV became so skilled in the idiosyncrasies of the law that he was now considered by most to be the king of environmental law in Vermont.

Louis IV married Maureen Phelps, the most popular girl in the BHS class of 1979. Her father was a successful attorney, and chairman of the board of directors of the Burlington Savings Bank.

Her mother's family, the DeWitt's had started the bank in the mid 1800's. Her standing in old Burlington society surpassed almost all others. One of the oldest buildings at UVM had been named after her Great Grandfather, William Clinton DeWitt. It was a marriage of power and influence.

Louis and Maureen bought a large house in the hill section of Burlington where they lived. They summered in a beautiful cottage they had built on the West Shore of Marble Island.

They had two children, both girls now in college. Louis IV's only shortcoming was to fail to have a male heir to carry on the O'Brien name.

Recently, Louis IV had returned the family to local political prominence by defeating the six term incumbent mayor by thirty-four votes. He had spent $250,000 on his campaign for a $65,000 a year job. It is not that he needed the money, or that the mayor's position was the powerful post that it had been in generations past.

Louis IV had a huge ego, and spending $41.66 for each vote he received did not really surprise Jack.

According to the political rumor mill, Louis IV's current office was merely a stepping-stone for his political ambitions. The current talk was that he was preparing to run for the

United States Senate in three years, when Senator Joseph Leddy was rumored to be retiring.

How did the just deceased Bennie Richards, little known mini mart owner, figure in to Louis IV's future plans? Why had he bothered to attend his wake?

CHAPTER 7

Jack Johnson's police career was the all-consuming passion of his life, or so his ex-wife had claimed when she asked Jack to leave their home and life together after twenty-five years of marriage.

Their split up and divorce surprised almost everyone who knew them, but no one more than Jack. Sally had become over time a successful Realtor. She wanted more out of life than being married to a cop.

The divorce became final just over five and a half years ago, It was just a few months later that he suffered a severe heart attack and underwent emergency by-pass surgery.

Jack's marriage and his police career started and ended at almost the same time. It only took six months of intensive physiological therapy to get over the marriage breaking up. He was still looking for a new career.

He had tried selling radio advertising, but he had not been able to get excited doing it, so he had quit after a few years.

After that, Jack had returned to his beginnings in a sense. Needing a place to live when his marriage went bust, he had bought an old houseboat. He kept it in a slip at Marble Island Marina.

The old hotel had burned down a dozen years before on a very cold February night. Conrad O'Brien, Charles' only child, had reluctantly assumed the post of owner/host of Marble Island when his father had retired. Conrad was never truly willing to embrace the hospitality industry as his career.

Since high school, Conrad had been much more interested in pretty girls, fast cars, and a quick hustle than to any kind of hard work. The modern playboy does not want to be tied down to a career in the service industry.

Conrad fancied himself a modern playboy. He had been engaged at least three times, each to a young woman in their early twenties. A marriage date was never set. After a time, the length depending on the intelligence (or lack of), the fiancé, they would give up on Conrad and move on to greener pastures.

Conrad's second fiancé hung on for almost six years before she finally realized that there would be no marriage. His current fiancé was a young woman for whom Conrad's first fiancé had babysat.

A few months after Charles passed away in December 1993, the old hotel went up in flames. The state fire marshal had determined that it had been an electrical short in one of the vacant guest rooms in the south wing that had started the fire.

As the fire occurred late on a subzero February night when the meeting rooms and south wing were closed, it smoldered for several hours during the late night before an employee discovered and reported it.

By the time the Colchester volunteer fire department arrived, the only things left were the golf course, tennis courts, pool, marina, and parking lot. Fortunately, the few hotel guests staying that night had been on the north wing of the building and escaped unharmed.

Rumors of arson abounded, but no evidence was uncovered to substantiate the accusations, and eventually the insurance company paid off for the blaze.

Conrad, freed from the responsibility of running a hotel, began to enjoy the life of a real estate mogul, developing the resort into an exclusive waterfront community. The real estate was much more valuable as building lots than as a hotel and golf course.

Jack was now working for the O'Brien family at Marble Island part-time again. He was the custodian at the marina. 39 years after his first term of employment he was working for the son of the man who hired his father.

In addition to the meager pay he got for overseeing the operation of the marina, Jack also received his slip and winter storage for the boat. His disability police pension took care of the groceries and other expenses, with barely enough left over to buy cigars.

In the winter months, Jack took care of his older brother Tom's house and dogs in South Hero while Tom and his wife Helen wintered in Florida. It was a good arrangement for both brothers.

CHAPTER 8

The morning sky was gray. The winds were from the southwest at 15 to 20 mph with higher gusts. Rain was in the forecast for the afternoon. It was not even a good day for fishing.

After Jack checked the docks for loose lines, cleaned the bathrooms, and dumped the trashcans at the marina he went to follow through on his promise to Jean Richards.

His first stop was a rendezvous with Vermont State Trooper Vince Talbot. Vince had started with the Burlington force before he moved over to the State Police, so Jack had known him for a while.

He was the trooper who discovered Bennies wrecked van in the Winooski River. Jack met him at 9:00 A.M. at the Williston Road Dunkin Donuts just off the Interstate.

They started with small talk over coffee about the morning's take on the perennial Interstate 89 speed traps. It was a slow day for Vince, which was good.

In the past few years there had been an increasing number of accidents due to heavy commuter traffic volume, and driver's road rage.

The state needed to bring things back under control. What better way than to start giving out tickets like they were free beads at Mardi gras for all moving violations.

In short order all the commuters expected the cops to be there and slowed down. So now, it took a lot fewer patrols to keep things flowing smoothly and more safely.

After the coffee and small talk, Vince and Jack got into the police cruiser and drove out to the accident scene at the Winooski River Bridge abutment. They parked the cruiser in the medium and got out to look around. Vince described the scene.

"There were no visible skid marks. The remains of the tire tracks in the grass went straight into the medium, through a temporary opening in the guard rails that had been opened up to allow work crews to perform maintenance on the bridge. They continued to the edge of the embankment overlooking the river."

Looking down from the edge, they could see the almost vertical drop to the river. There were a few spots visible where the van had scraped the rocks on the way down.

Vince commented "it was almost amazing that the path of the van had been so precise."

"Bennie had to be either asleep, passed out, or dead not to have tried to stop or swerve. With no witness's and no contrary evidence, the only reasonable explanation was that he fell asleep and drove off the road."

"If he had been wearing his seat belt, he might have survived."

They returned to Dunkin Donuts. Jack thanked Vince and got into his truck, and proceeded to his next stop, the state medical examiners' office/ morgue.

It was located in the basement level of the Fletcher Allen Health Care complex. Unlike most departments in the hospital, it was not part of the 1.3 billion plus dollar Renaissance project that had just been completed.

It seemed that few people were concerned with the accommodations for those who are already dead. Parking had received more attention in the renovations than the morgue.

The Renaissance Project had been the grand name attached to the massive redesign of Fletcher Allen Health Care. The renovations huge cost overruns were Burlington's latest scandal.

When the Vermont State Public Service Board had approved the expansion project, the public and board were told that the cost would be $500 million. That amount turned out to be less than half the true total.

Over half way through the three year project a local newspaper reporter discovered that the immense new parking garage costs had been left out of the public figure. The true expense was more than double what had been disclosed. All hell had broken loose.

The board of directors quickly adopted the stance that management had misinformed them, just as they had the public. After a highly publicized investigation into the scandal, the chief operating officer of FAHC went to prison.

The chief financial officer paid a large fine and was placed on probation. The chair of the board of directors resigned along with three other members. The Chair was Louis O'Brien IV.

Burlington being a small town, the head of the morgue, Dr. Grant Peterson and Jack were friends of a sort. Grant's wife's father and Jack's ex-wife's father had been roommates at the YMCA when they had arrived in Burlington in the mid thirties.

More than once Grant and Jack kept each other company during boring family parties and weddings, when their spouses had brought them along and then abandoned them for the crowd.

Grant's review of his examination had revealed little more that Vince had told Jack.

"Bennie died of massive head and neck injuries. His head must have slammed into the roof and windshield pillar when the front end of his van hit the bottom of the shallow water under the bridge. His death was instantaneous."

"There was no water in his lungs to indicate he had survived the initial impact. His neck was broken in two different places. The first break was at the base of his skull where you would expect from the sudden snap of the head backwards after impacting the pillar. The second break was just above his shoulders."

"Apparently, something in the back of the van flew forward and slammed into him upon impact. Either of these breaks would have caused his instant death by themselves as they both completely severed the spinal cord. All of his blood work came back clean. There was no trace of drugs or alcohol. Bennie Richards died excessively."

CHAPTER 9

Andrews Salvage and Towing was located in the entrance to Burlington's Intervale. It was another piece of Burlington's history in a way. In the fifties, a new small wave of immigrants started to make their way to Burlington. They were Lebanese Christian families who were seeking a better opportunity in America than was available in their homeland.

Like the Irish immigrants of the late 1800's, some of them discovered Burlington and decided to make it their home. On the advice of the immigration officer at Ellis Island where he entered his new country, one of the first to settle in Burlington had chosen the American name Samuel Andrews to put on his paperwork when he immigrated. He quickly became known by a shortened version of his new name, Sam.

Sam was a mechanical genius. He could repair a car with bubble gum and baling twine, according to Jack's ex-wife's late father. He started a garage on this piece of then worthless property overlooking the Burlington dump.

He brought over his brothers and cousins as quickly as they could get their immigration papers. They worked hard at the jobs no one else wanted to do. They collected the garbage. They worked in the sewer plant. No task was beneath them. Everything was an opportunity.

The only quirk in their nature was the family feuds that would arise between them over minor incidents. Sam and his cousin George had not talked to each other since 1963 when George forgot to send Sam's infant daughter a birthday gift.

To this day, they would cross the street to avoid contact with each other.

Sam now owned over thirty mini marts, twenty neighborhood stores, and well over a hundred apartment units in the Burlington area. His base of operations remained upstairs in the little garage he had built fifty years ago.

He was an old man now and his sons ran the business. However, he still came in every day, and knew every decision made.

His younger cousin George was in the wholesale grocery, beer, and cigarette business. He distributed mostly to stores and mini marts just like the thirty that Sam owned and operated.

Sam Andrews would not have anything to do with George and did business with a St. Albans wholesale business to get his supplies.

It was widely known that Sam had said many times that when the time came, he would spit on George's grave.

George responded that he planned to do the same for Sam if he outlived him.

George also ran the still highly profitable trash collection business that had been started by both cousins together before their feud.

His son-in-law, Bob Brendon, oversaw the daily operations so that George could concentrate on the wholesale grocery enterprise.

Joe Andrews, one of Sam's sons, had been one of Jack's classmates in high school. After a short conversation, Joe let him into the fenced impound area with a warning not to mess anything up, as the contract with the state was a lucrative one.

It was where the fatal wrecks were stored until investigations were completed. The vehicles were supposed to be strictly off limits to everyone but police officials.

The van was typical Bennie Richards. It was an eight year old green Dodge Grand Caravan. The name of his store appeared nowhere on it.

That allowed Bennie to drive it anywhere without standing out. Bennie really could not afford another car, and did not want to be embarrassed when he went out socially by being seen driving a work vehicle.

The front end of the vehicle was pushed in as expected. The driver's side of the roof was crushed as well. Chrysler built a tough van though. The slider on the passenger side opened quite nicely.

A quick check of the interior showed the dual purposes that it had served. The second seat was in place and the third removed to make room for the inventory Bennie was picking up.

His few personal items had been thrown all over the interior. A coffee mug and several flattened cigarette packages, as well as an empty soda can. As Jack had expected there seemed nothing out of the ordinary to find.

When he finished looking at the van, he went back in the garage to thank Joe. Sam saw him and asked "What are you up to Jack? Are you in the private investigation business now?"

"Not really, as a favor to an old family friend I was checking Bennie Richards' van for personal effects for his mother. It doesn't take a detective to do that."

"Well, please extend my condolences to Jean, she's a good person and didn't deserve this tragedy. Parents should not have to bury their children. It's supposed to be the other way around."

"I will Sam, I'm sure she will appreciate your thinking of her."

Jack had decided that there was no reason to arouse anyone's suspicions about the accident. That was how rumors got started.

"Bennie was a good man", Sam said. "He had asked me for advice on how to set up his mini mart after his dad died. I helped him get his mini mart set up and gave him one piece of advice that he always followed. Do not do any business with my cousin George Andrews. He's a crook."

Jack said goodbye and left.

CHAPTER 10

It was late afternoon when Jack finished checking out Bennie's van at Andrews Garage. The Channel Four weather team had done their usual incorrect forecast of the weather.

The sun was shining and the wind had died out around noontime. There was not a cloud to be seen. He decided to go down to the waterfront and have a cold beer before he went back to Marble Island.

Jack went to an outdoor Restaurant/Bar named Breakers. From mid May to Labor Day, it was one of the busiest watering spots in Burlington.

It sat at the end of the ferry dock on the manmade fill that made up the waterfront in the heart of Burlington Bay. You could look out at the breakwater, back at the city on the hill, down to Shelburne Bay or just enjoy seeing the sunset over the Adirondacks.

This afternoon Jack was just going to enjoy being outside. He ordered his beer of choice, a Molson Excel. It was nonalcoholic. Jack had not had a real beer or any other alcoholic beverage in 12 years.

That's when he had realized how empty his marriage had become. Being married to his ex-wife Sally had evolved into like living with a close friend. There had not been any intimacy between them during the last several years of their marriage.

Jack had started drinking a lot and enjoying it little. He came to realize how depressed he was, and how he was using alcohol as a crutch to try to escape his depression.

Sally's father had been an alcoholic. His drinking and behavior relating to it had blown out any flames that had ever existed in his marriage to her mother.

Jack had felt he had done the same thing to Sally in their marriage. He knew if he stopped drinking, things would get better again. Jack had gotten married to Sally for forever.

He did what he thought was right and quit drinking. He felt that it would change and reinvigorate their relationship and bring back the closeness that they had once felt for each other. It had not changed anything. Their relationship became more distant instead of closer.

Jack did come to realize how much the alcohol had slowed down his thought process. After he'd quit drinking he found that he could do a much better job at work, so he started working a lot more and going home a lot less. Days off were spent golfing with friends, doing chores around the house, or going off alone to sail on their sloop.

Sally and Jack became strangers living together because neither of them knew how to end the marriage. Sally went on long vacations with her mother and brother. Jack would use his for sailing vacations on the lake with his brothers.

After living like that for six years after Jack had quit drinking, Sally had left him a note on the kitchen counter saying that she needed to take a break from their marriage. He had packed some clothes and gone to stay with his sister.

Jack was sipping on his beer thinking of this. He lit up one of his cigars and started to let his mind drift to more pleasant things when someone tapped him on the shoulder.

He said "I'm sorry if the cigar smoke is bothering you, I'll move to another table where it doesn't invade your space" before he even turned around. Even outdoors, smoking was becoming more and more of a hassle.

The shoulder tapper laughed and asked Jack "Do you have an extra cigar?" Jack turned around and saw the mayor standing behind him.

Louis O'Brien IV sat down with his drink, and Jack handed him his last Fuente. He decided to claim its value as a political contribution.

As the Johnson family enjoyed very little political or social prominence, and Jack was not even a Burlington resident anymore, he was not sure why Louis IV would single him out to sit with, especially when Jack was doing something as politically incorrect as smoking in public.

Perhaps the mayor wanted to be seen publicly partaking in something as minor a sin as smoking. After all, most notable politicians Jack could remember had at least one picture taken with a cigar in their mouth.

The best way to find out what Louis wanted was to listen.

Louis asked him "What's the story on Bennie Richards' accident.

Jack could not imagine why the mayor would have any interest.

He decided to tell Louis of his current quest, "At the request of Jean Richards, I did some checking today and it seems that it was just that, an accident. It's not really much of a story. He apparently fell asleep and went off the road and into the river."

After a little more small talk about Jack's current health status, Jack decided return the conversation to Bennie Richards' death.

"So Louis, why did you go to Bennie's wake?

The Mayor's reply was "Because Bennie's mother had worked for the O'Brien family for many years. It seemed appropriate that an O'Brien would attend to extend the family's condolences to an old and valued employee who had tragically lost her only child."

"That's nice Louis but since I never you at or near the resort when it was operating, perhaps it would have been more meaningful to Bennie's family if your cousin Conrad had been the one to attend on your family's behalf. I know that his plate isn't too full right now, or did you forget that I work for him?"

Louis' reaction to his suggestion was to lower his eyes like someone who had been caught in a lie.

It made Jack think that respect for Jean Richards had not been the motivation for the mayor's attendance. What other reason could there be?

John Patch

Louis didn't need the votes. It was highly unlikely that there would be any increase in donations to his political fund. There was no press coverage at the funeral service. He could think of no good reason.

A group of three local business owners rescued Jack from the mayor. They came over to the table and sat down to discuss "important city business" with him. Jack excused himself and left for his boat/home.

The sunset would be just as beautiful from the upper deck of Jack's houseboat as from the Burlington lakefront anyway, and the company would be more stimulating than the three self-important men buttonholing the mayor to try to further their own agendas.

CHAPTER 11

Jack got back to his houseboat, threw a frozen Chicken Kiev into the microwave oven for dinner, grabbed an Excel from the refrigerator, and went out on the upper deck to watch the sunset and review his day.

He had not really discovered very much, nor had he expected to. The only mystery in the day was why Louis O'Brien seemed interested in the circumstances of Bennie Richards' death. Maybe Jack was missing something. What was it?

When he went over all the information again in his mind, Jack realized that not everything about the accident was as routine as it first appeared. The lack of skidding or swerving was not normal in an accident when the driver fell asleep.

If Bennie had dozed off as everyone assumed it would have only been a few moments before he went into the medium. The change in sound and feel should have awakened him. Bennie's first reaction would have been to hit the brakes and turn the wheel.

Then there were the scrape marks from the van on the rocks going down the bank. If the van had gone over the embankment at 50 plus miles an hour, it should have landed in the middle of the river, not as near the edge as it did, and it certainly should not have scraped on the way down.

Where was the heavy object that flew forward into Bennie and broke his neck just above his shoulders? What kind of detective was Jack to have missed this?

He was going to bring these inconsistencies to the attention of the state police in the morning. It should extend the investigation for at least a few days.

CHAPTER 12

Vermont State Police "A Barracks" was located just off from Interstate 89 exit 12 on Route 2A in Williston. Barracks commander Captain John Leonard was not pleased with Jack's questions.

Leonard's highest priority was to slow down interstate traffic to legal posted limits and reduce the number of accidents occurring, so the federal government did not withhold any potential highway funds.

He did not want or need a questionable death in a car accident to pull resources from that priority. He quickly reviewed the report that Trooper Vince Talbot had submitted.

The accident had occurred on the Interstate. However, it was technically in the city of Burlington at the base of the bridge over the Winooski River.

Captain Leonard thought that if there were questions regarding the circumstances, the Burlington police department should take the lead on the case. He was diplomatically telling Jack that he was not going to do any additional follow up on the accident.

Jack had an uncomfortable feeling that he would not be welcomed with open arms at his alma mater. He had been a very good cop in the trenches, and an outspoken critic of the way the department was run.

It was more like a public relations firm than a Police Department. The chief spent more time working on Rotary Club committee meetings than on running the department.

His department heads were political allies recruited from outside the department instead of deserved promotions from the ranks.

As a result, most of the recruits who took a position with the Burlington police department did so for the higher initial pay and training.

Then, just as State Trooper Vince Talbot had done years before, they jumped to another department when the first opportunity came along.

It made for low morale in the ranks, and few truly experienced officers on the force. That combined with the lack of skilled supervision due to the political nature of advancement made the few veterans who did stay with the Burlington department and try to change things very unpopular with the brass.

Jack had been one of their ringleaders. Anything that he brought to them would be viewed with skepticism. Jack knew it was going to be a very hard sell.

Chief Michael Kelly was the stereotype of the Irish cop. He even sang tenor in his church choir, and did a magnificent solo of Danny Boy each year at the Rotary luncheon for St. Patrick's Day.

He was close friends with George Andrews who was the chair of the Burlington Police Commission. The new Police Station had been paid for through the generosity of Andrews after the voters had turned down a bond issue.

George had bought the property, an old auto dealership, adjacent to Battery Park and renovated it to the specifications the police chief had wanted and that the voters had declined to fund with a bond issue.

He then leased it to the city for a 99-year term for $1.00 per year with the only caveat being that it would revert to George's possession if the Police Department ever moved from the location.

It was a move that insured Andrews' position as chair of the Police Commission for as long as he chose to be there. The city quickly sold the old police building and put the cash into their general fund.

Jack waited for just over an hour before the chief saw him. He quickly reviewed the details of the accident report and initial investigation by the State Police.

He then pointed out to the chief the lack of skid marks or swerving, the injuries found in the autopsy, and the lack of any object that could have broken Bennie's neck.

Chief Kelly listened politely. When Jack had finished he agreed with him that there might be a few inconsistencies and perhaps even a few unanswered questions that were not addressed in the investigation report.

"Few accidents make perfect sense, that's why they're called traffic accidents and not traffic incidents" the chief commented. "I'll review the report with my captain of detectives and determine if there is merit to pursuing any additional investigation."

"That's great Chief Kelly. I appreciate the accommodation. I'll give you a few days and check back in with you. I've taken enough of your time today. Thanks again for seeing me."

Chief Kelly replied, "Johnson, I'll have someone get in touch with you if there is any need, you needn't bother to call the department as we are all very busy right now."

CHAPTER 13

It was time to go and see Jean Richards. Jack had done the job she had asked him to do. Now it was up to the police as to whether or not there would be any additional investigation into Bennie's death. Jack did not have a lot of faith that they would decide to do any.

There was no hard evidence to back up his questions, only his feelings and some unconnected dots. Bennie had not been important enough. There was not any apparent motive.

No one had gained from his death. Only Bennie and his family had lost. It was tragic, but was it any more than an accident with a few unanswered questions?

Jack stopped by the mini mart. The lunch rush was over at the deli counter. Jean was cleaning up the grill. She stopped working when she saw him.

She told her daughter-in-law Terry who was working at the cash register that she would be out back having a smoke. As soon as they were outside, she asked what Jack had found out.

"There are a few questions about the accident but no hard evidence. I went first to the state police and then to the Burlington police with my concerns. The state cops passed it off immediately to Burlington. The Burlington Police Department will probably decide that there's not enough there to pursue."

Although disappointed Jean did not seem surprised. "What will happen now? Where will it go from here?"

Jack replied "If the Burlington Police Department decides not to investigate further it will go nowhere except in a closed case file under traffic fatality. Have you been able to think of anything more as to what Bennie's information was or to whom it pertained?"

"I haven't a clue as to what the information was but I might know where Bennie would have kept it."

"He spent a lot of time on his computer at the house late at night. Terry thought he was cruising pornographic sights, but Bennie wasn't like that".

"He must have been researching something. He was always looking for little things that had been overlooked in news stories. Bennie really didn't like the job the Free Press did reporting the news. He thought they were very lax about facts."

Jack knew this about Bennie already, as did anyone who read the letters to the editor. He had been a regular writer, usually ranting about the inaccuracies and omissions in local news stories, especially if the inclusion of these items would bring about any embarrassment to politically or socially prominent individuals. Sour grapes, Jack figured.

"Jean, I'll be in touch if I hear anything else." He went back inside and bought a Pastrami on Rye and a diet ice tea for lunch and left.

CHAPTER 14

Jack felt like all he had accomplished with his investigation so far was to add to Jean Richards's grief and perhaps give her false hope. She was looking for closure, and he could have given it to her simply by telling her that the facts did not show anything contrary to his having died in a traffic accident.

Instead, he had prolonged it by sharing his questions with her. He told himself he needed to take a refresher course on compassion.

He decided to take his boat out and see if he could catch anything besides perch on his favorite reef. There might even be a couple of large Walleye waiting for him. He stopped by the bait shop on his way back to the marina to pick up some crawlers.

A 36-foot houseboat is not a typical fishing boat on Lake Champlain, but it was what Jack had, so he went back to the marina and cast off.

…You have to use what you have in order to get what you want… was a piece of wisdom that Jack's dad had espoused. It had never made much sense to Jack, but it seemed to fit today.

Fishing time was Jack's time to think about his dad. They had pulled pretty far apart when Jack was a teenager. His father constantly told him that he had champagne taste and a beer pocketbook.

Jack had bought as his first car, a late model Chevy Malibu Super Sport, instead of the VW beetle that his dad had recommended. He had partied too much, spent too much and saved too little.

Jack knew now that Newell had been so critical of him because he had cared, but at the time, it seemed like he could not accept that Jack could take care of his own life, or thought he could anyway.

It was the same with all of Jack's siblings and their dad. It was hard for Newell to let them jump out of the nest so that they could learn to fly.

When Jack came home from the Navy, he and his father had started to get along again. Newell had become Jack's best and closest friend.

Newell Johnson had died of a massive heart attack in November 1978. He was the most honest and sincere man Jack had ever met. There had not been a bigoted or racist bone in his body.

In the hotel business, the employees covered the racial spectrum from black to white and everything in between.

Gay or straight, citizen, green card holder, or illegal immigrant, everyone was the same to Jack's father.

He had preached it to his children and his employees ....Everyone had a job to do.... If you did it well you were a good person... If you worked for Newell Johnson and you did not then you were let go.

Newell had told Jack many times that you were not helping someone who was not doing their job by keeping them. It was not fair to the house, to the other employees, or to the guests at the hotel.

Newell's love and commitment to Jack's mother, his children, his family, and his career was reflected in everything he did.

He was a sixth generation Vermonter whose ancestors included veterans from every war back to the American Revolution, so leaving the state for a higher paying job had been out of the question.

Even the 70 mile move north to Burlington was hard for him because his own siblings were still in Rutland. The economic opportunities in Rutland had dried up with the bankrupt Rutland Railroad in the mid 1960's.

When the two hotels that he had managed for the Goldstein family for over 20 years were being sold to a large chain, he sought out another family to work for. The O'Brien's of Burlington seemed like the best fit to him.

He'd moved his family north and given the O'Brien's his total loyalty for 12 years until the moment of his death in a corridor at the Marble Island resort.

Newell's cardiologist had assured Jack that his dad had been dead before he hit the floor. There had been no suffering.

Charles O'Brien had returned that loyalty to Newell and Jack's mother Myrtle. After the funeral Charles had given Myrtle a large check.

It was from a life insurance policy that he had taken out on Jack's father because he had been the key man in the operation at Marble Island. Charles had wanted her to have it.

Newell was only 64 years old when he died, and having raised six kids, he and Jack's mom hadn't been able to put away much for retirement. Now she was able to winter in Naples Florida in a modest home. It had been made possible by Charles' generosity.

Newell Johnson did quote many sayings that made good sense. He lived by the golden rule. ...Do unto others, as you would have them do unto you... Over time, Jack had learned to live by believing in another ...What goes around comes around...

The Walleyes weren't biting this afternoon, at least not on night crawlers. That was all right. Jack was enjoying the company, just himself and his memories of his father.

Life was good sometimes, Jack loved the lake, and he was able to live on it. He had a good cigar and a cold Excel at his side. Now, if he could just get rid of the nagging feeling that there was more to Bennie's death than he was seeing.

CHAPTER 15

A week went by with no message from the Burlington police chief. Jack's gut had been right. There was not going to be an investigation. Jean called him and asked him to stop by the house to look at Bennie's computer.

Jack did not feel like he could say no to her, even though he doubted that he would find out anything significant to Bennie's accident. When she said dinner was included, they set it up for the following evening.

When Jack arrived at 6 P.M., Bennie's widow Terry and their kids were not home. They had decided to visit her parents for a long weekend and had left for Orleans in the northeast kingdom right after school had gotten out.

Jean had remembered that Jack was a steak and potatoes lover. She asked him to start the grill on the back patio while she checked the twice-baked potatoes in the oven. She even had an Excel poured in a cold schooner for him. It was like visiting his mom in Florida.

The view of the waterfront from the back yard was much nicer than it had been in the 1960's and 1970's. There had been a rebirth of the once rundown and overgrown area.

The only reminder left of the "old days" was the Moran Generating Plant skeleton with windows broken out of it and graffiti covering its sides as far up as kids can reach.

Many of the warehouses had been restored and converted to office and living space. Burlington had developed a beautiful park with a floating boathouse for area residents to enjoy.

After dinner, Jean took Jack into Bennie's office, a small enclosed porch on the north side of the house. She turned on the computer and left him with another Excel to peruse the files and see what he could find.

It was mostly what he had expected. There was a complete record of Bennie's many ranting letters to the editor. An attachment to each letter was the "proof" that there were errors and omissions in the various articles he was complaining about.

Terry had been at least partially correct in that Bennie had visited a few porn sites. Jack would not bother to mention that to Jean, he just erased the file that they were in.

Then Jack found a file named "Quandaries". When he opened it up, he found several old Free Press articles that had been scanned in. The oldest of them going back as far as the late 1960's.

Most of them had to do with various unsolved crimes that had been committed over the years. There were also a few that referred to solved cases.

John Patch

There were several about the arsonist that had burned down several churches and old warehouse buildings in the 1970's.

The Burlington police had apprehended one person at the scene of a church fire with minor burns on his hands and face; a gasoline can in the trunk of his car, and several matchbooks in his pockets.

He was an unbalanced college kid. He pled innocent by reason of insanity, and after a psychological examination had been performed by state doctors was sent to the State Mental Hospital in Waterbury where he remained today.

A few of the police involved in the investigation, including Jack, had felt that the young man was only responsible for the last fire, copying the methodology from the original arsonist who had never been identified.

The department brass had decided otherwise and announced that the person responsible for all of the fires was no longer free to continue on his rampage. The public was declared safe from future fires.

As there had been no more big fires set in the same manner, over time Jack had to admit that apparently the brass had been right.

Several articles were about Mary Robbins, the schoolteacher who had disappeared in 1978. This disappearance had been the first big case Jack had worked on after receiving his promotion to detective.

The Shelburne police department was a three man operation in 1978. They had asked the Burlington police department for help and the Burlington Police Department had sent him.

Mary Robbins had been at home the day that she had disappeared. She had been a school teacher. It was exam week and she had no exams to give that day. One of the neighbors had seen her leaving for her daily walk late in the morning. No one had seen or heard from her since.

Gary Robbins had not reported her missing until the day after her disappearance when he got home from work.

He later claimed that they had argued before he had left for work the morning before when she had told him she was going to stay with a friend overnight so she could think about things.

Because of the argument, when he got home that night after work and she was not there, he did not think anything of it.

He had not asked her whom the friend was that she was staying with and did not know. No friend of Mary's came forward to back up this claim.

The school had called Gary at work the following day when Mary had failed to show up to give her scheduled exams and not answered the phone when they had called her. Gary told the principal she was sick in bed when he had left for work. He had forgotten to call in for her.

When the police first confronted him with this, Gary claimed that he had lied to cover up that she had stayed with a friend the previous night because he did not want anyone to know they had argued.

He had been certain that she would call the high school before the end of the day, and be home when he arrived for dinner that evening. It all seemed a bit too contrived to believe.

The police felt that Robbins had motive. He and Mary were arguing quite a bit according to friends and neighbors.

He was stayed out late regularly and running around rather indiscriminately. Mary's mother had said that Mary had been hinting about leaving him.

His alibi then became that he had gone out with the boys after work. He became too drunk to drive home so he had crashed on a friend's couch. His friends, trying to help him out, at first had lied for him regarding the company he kept that night.

Eventually, the bartender at the last bar Robbins had visited confirmed that he did not leave until a little after midnight.

He left with a young lady who definitely was not his wife. After a quick romp in the back of his car, she went home alone before 2:00 A.M.

Once the police had established that Gary could not account for his whereabouts after 2:00 A.M. on the night of the 23rd it appeared that he had the time, as well as the motive, to kill her and dispose of the body.

The following September, having been unable to find any incriminating evidence without a body, they had even excavated around his house, throughout the neighborhood, and in the wooded area leading to the beach on the end of Shelburne Point where she had taken her daily walks looking for her body. They never found her.

The oldest article was from the Boston Herald. It had to do with a stolen cigarette tax machine, used by the State of Vermont to mark the packages sold in the state.

It had been stolen one night from a warehouse in Montpelier Vt. in the late 1960's. A security guard had been badly injured during the theft. A stolen truck matching the description of the one used in the heist had turned up outside of Boston in the warehouse district of the harbor area.

An unknown person's fingerprints found at the crime scene matched some found in the cab of the truck. The machine had disappeared. The case was considered at a dead end.

A few years later, a break came in the case when several storeowners in southern Vermont were found to be selling cigarettes that had been stamped by the stolen machine. The Federal Bureau of Alcohol, Tobacco and Firearms set up a sting operation.

The bust came in Boston because that was where the cigarette distributor who had been supplying the southern Vermont stores was located. It was determined to be a front for an organized crime operation. The tax stamp machine was never recovered.

There must have been a tip off about the pending raid on the distributor and it had been disposed of by the thieves who were using it to prevent its use as evidence. That case was closed with everyone feeling good about it.

Jack emailed a copy of Bennie's "Quandaries" file to himself so he could download it on his laptop. Bennie had apparently thought there was more to these cases to be found out. Jack was not sure that there was, but he had the time to look at them.

Finding nothing else, he turned off Bennie's computer and went back into the living room where Jean was sitting. He told her that he had not found anything that helped find Bennie's somebody.

It was time for her to let it go. She handed Jack a cardboard box with a bunch of photos in it that Bennie had taken over the years, explaining that a few weeks ago he had pulled it out of the basement and started going through it.

Most of the photos were personal. Other pictures were dated on the back. They were from when Bennie's dad was still alive. They were of cars that Bennie had towed for the service station when he had worked for his dad.

Jack asked Jean "Why would Bennie take pictures of the cars that he towed?

She explained "A lot of people who had their cars towed because they parked illegally claimed bogus damage had been caused to their vehicles by the tow truck operators.

"Photos showing the condition of the cars prior to them being towed helped eliminate these bogus claims. The photographic evidence shut down most complaints immediately. Bennies dad had taught him never to hook up to a car until after he had taken pictures of it. We threw the pictures out after the owners paid for their cars. I'm not sure why Bennie would have saved these."

It was an interesting bit of trivial knowledge for Jack, and reminded him of another of his dad's sayings... A picture is worth a thousand words. The cops version of that was ... don't tell me, show me.

Jack was not sure what if any significance the photos had, but Jean insisted that he take them with him. He finally agreed and told her he would have them back to her in a few days. As he had hoped, she suggested that he bring them back to the house, and she would cook dinner for him again.

CHAPTER 16

The next morning at the marina Conrad O'Brien came down on the docks and found Jack at 7:30 A.M.

"Jack, I've decided to restore the old Donzi. I'd like to have it ready to go in time to participate in the Burlington antique boat parade on July 4th. Pull it out of the boat shed and start on it as soon as you have time."

"You're the boss Conrad. I'm surprised with your sudden passion for antique boats. The Donzi's been in the shed for so long I almost forgot that it's there. I'm amazed that you even remember you own it."

"Tiffany was impressed with some old pictures of it that she found in an album that was laying around the house. I told her that the boat is ten years older than she is. I want to surprise her by having it in the water for her birthday which happens to fall on the 4th of July."

"It's a good thing for you that she likes old things, Conrad. I can get started on it today. How much time and money do you want to put into this project. To do it right is going to be several thousand dollars."

"Spend what it takes to do it right. I can always sell it when Tiffany loses interest. It's actually a rare boat to have, so I'm sure that I'll be able to recover my investment and turn a profit."

Conrad currently owned a 36 foot Lafountain go fast boat with twin big block Chevrolet motors. He raced around on it each summer to keep up his "Miami Vice" image.

The Donzi had belonged to Conrad's father and Uncle Louis III since it was new in the early 1970's. They had kept it on a dock at the Shelburne Shipyard marina, so Conrad and Louis IV could use it without having to drive out to Malletts Bay and then motor the 17 miles by water back to Burlington harbor.

The boys had used it regularly for water skiing with their friends. Conrad and Louis IV had been very competitive on the slalom course that they used in front of Maureen Phelps grandparents house on Shelburne Point. The competition was not just about who was the better water skier.

Both had their sights set on Maureen Phelps. Louis had eventually won, but only after she came to realize Conrad's commitment issues the hard way. She found out he was cheating when Louis had proven it to her.

Charles had bought out his brother's interest in the Donzi after the kids had gone to college. He moved it out to Marble Island, where he used almost daily every summer to cruise around Malletts Bay.

Since his death in 1992, the boat sat in back corner of the old boat shed covered by a tarp and forgotten.

Thank God, the boat was fiberglass or it would have been a lost cause. It was not that it would not be worth quite of money when it was restored; Jack thought as he pulled it out of its corner into the work area of the shed and pulled off the tarp.

This was going to be a project. The field mice had had a hey-day with the interior cushions and upholstery. The carpet was mildewed and stained well beyond use. He could only imagine what the cost of this little project would be.

Conrad told him to do it right. Jack contacted an upholsterer to start on the interior and took off the engine cover to start on the mechanicals.

Every hose and belt was suffering from dry rot, the engine had seized from rust, and the propeller shaft was quite corroded. Nothing several thousand dollars would not take care of.

Jack decided that he would rebuild the motor himself. It was a small block Ford. He would take the transmission down to Lake George and leave it to be rebuilt at a repair shop that specialized in Donzi boats. While they were going through it, Jack would replace the plywood floor and install new carpet.

Another of Jack's father's sayings came to his mind…the difference between men and boys is the sound of their voice and the cost of their toys… his own version was… you've got to pay to play…

CHAPTER 17

Jack worked on the Donzi until mid-afternoon pulling out the motor and transmission. After a shower to wash off the grime, he made a quick trip to the local Shaw's supermarket to pick up some groceries.

Jack ran into his sister Carol at the store and asked her if she would like to go out to outer Malletts Bay near the railroad fill on the boat, grill some salmon for dinner and watch the sunset.

They agreed that she would bring wine for herself, seeing that he did not have any on board and she did not like beer.

Carol was Jack's port in the storm. She is the oldest of his siblings closing in on her 57th birthday. She had married when she was 18 years old, just out of high school in 1966.

Newell had insisted that she would make the move to Burlington with the rest of the family. Her only way to stay in Rutland was to get married.

Her husband Jim had been several years older than she was, and had very different values than she had grown up with. She stayed married to him for thirteen years rather that admit to Newell that she had made a mistake.

After he had died in 1978, she divorced from Jim and took an apartment in Rutland. Jack had talked her into moving to Burlington a few years later.

She had a good job with the Federal Court System and had been able transfer up to the Burlington Court. She bought a condominium in town and settled into the area nicely.

When Jack's marriage had broken up, he had stayed with Carol for the first six months. Even now, when Jack needed to talk with someone, or just be quiet with someone, she was his choice.

After dinner, while they were watching the sunset, Jack told Carol about the whole Bennie Richards thing.

She asked "Jack, what is your gut saying to you.

Another of his father's wisdoms was to … always to go with your gut… It had mostly served Jack well through the years. Now his sister was voicing his dad's advice.

Jack thought about this for a few minutes before replying

"Carol, my gut isn't sure yet, but my heart tells me that I need to pursue this. Only after I've done my best to answer the questions that have come up about the circumstances of the accident will I feel that I have done right by Jean Richards."

They got back to the docks at 9:00 P.M. Carol left to go home. Jack pulled out the box of Bennie's photos that he had brought back from Jean's house and started looking through them for anything that seemed to stick out.

The personal pictures were of Bennie's family. Jack did not spot anything that gave even the slightest clue as to who the mysterious somebody or what the mysterious something that he was looking for was. He quickly set them aside.

Then Jack arranged the towing photos in chronological order, and starting with oldest gave them a look over. He got to several that were marked May 23, 1978. Something was familiar about that date.

It was the day that Mary Robbins had disappeared. Bennie had written a question on the back of one of the photos … where did they go?… not much help. The pictures showed the Richards Gulf Station tow truck and several illegally parked cars on the side of Shelburne Point Road in front of the beach, which wound around the end of Shelburne Point in the background.

Jack remembered that it had been an unusually warm spring so there were many early season sunbathers. The beach on the roadside had been used for years by kids and local families to swim and hang out.

If you waded around to the end of the point, there was another small beach that was unofficially recognized as the nude beach for the Burlington area.

There was a bicycle and walking path on the other side of the point near the Shelburne Shipyard that gave easier access to the end of the point.

The town road had been posted in 1977 with no parking signs to try to chase the swimmers and sunbathers off.

It was the result of the homeowners from the small new development across the road from the beach. They actually owned only part of the beach property but were determined to make all of it private.

That development was where Mary and Gary Robbins house was located. The last confirmed sighting of Mary had been a neighbor who seen her going for her daily walk on the path headed toward the end of the point at around noon that day.

Had Bennie known something about her disappearance? Why wouldn't he have come forward? The police had exhausted all available leads in that case at the time.

They knew it must have been her husband who was responsible for her disappearance and probable death. He was the only person with motive. They just could not prove what had happened to her.

Jack could not imagine that Bennie Richards would not have shared anything that he had discovered with the police. That case was all that anyone talked about for months.

It remained a frequent item of speculation even now. The prominence of the Robbins family in Burlington guaranteed it.

Information that helped in solving the case would have made whoever came forward with it a hometown hero. It also would have earned them a fifty thousand dollar reward offered by the Robbins family.

Bennie Richards never would have let that opportunity pass. He just was not wired that way.

Jack decided he would look through everything on Bennie's computer again when he returned the photos. If there was anything in there regarding the disappearance, he had missed it.

CHAPTER 18

The next morning, Jack loaded the transmission and propeller shaft assembly from the Donzi into the back of his old Ford Ranger pickup. He also copied down the serial number from the motor so he could order the parts to rebuild it.

It was a nice day to drive down to Lake George, New York. It was about a two hour trip each way which allowed for plenty of time to think.

Jack still had Bennie's photos on his mind. What did the message …where did they go... mean? The first thing to figure out was whom he had been referring to. A closer look at the photos might help.

He could run the old plate numbers through a friend at the Vermont DMV, and talk to the car owners that were still reachable. Jack knew from being involved with the original investigation that the police had had not talked to Bennie Richards, or anyone who had their car towed that day about the case. It had not come up in the original investigation.

Before Jack went back to Chief Kelly or Captain Leonard about Bennie's accident, he wanted solid information. He knew that neither of their departments would lift a finger without it. It seemed like a long shot at best.

Just like "Cold Case" on television sometimes new evidence comes up a long time after a crime is committed that helps to solve it.

If Bennie had stumbled onto something and approached someone who had been involved in the disappearance, it could be a very strong motive for them to arrange an accident for him.

He would visit Robbins Auto Parts to order the engine rebuild parts for the Donzi. While Jack was there, he could chat with Gary.

He should be happy to help in any way he could. Jack hoped that he might recollect something that would shed some light on what, if any importance the photos had.

Throughout the investigation, Gary Robbins had continued to proclaim his innocence. The $50,000 reward offer for information leading to the arrest and conviction of the guilty party(s) was still being offered by him and his family.

Gary was desperate for redemption. Even now, twenty seven years later, very few people who knew him believed Gary Robbins was innocent. All Jack needed now was some proof of what had happened.

Jack returned from Lake George and picked up the May 23 photos from his boat. He dropped them off at The Photo

Garden on College Street, ordering enlargements of each of them.

He then went to the North Winooski Avenue branch of Robbins Auto Parts where the corporate office was and where he would be most likely to find Gary Robbins who had taken over as president of the company a few years earlier.

He gave the counter man the list of parts he wanted, along with the serial number of the motor. It would take about ½ hour to pull the parts that were in stock and order the others. Jack went to talk with Gary while he was waiting.

He had decided to keep everything casual for now. He did not want Gary Robbins or anyone else to jump to any conclusions about his questions.

Jack had interrogated Robbins several times about his wife's disappearance during the active investigation, so they were familiar with each other.

One of things Jack had learned about interrogating people was to try to keep them at ease and treat them respectfully. It came from another of his father's bits of wisdom …you can catch more flies with honey than with vinegar…

As a result of this, even though he thought Robbins was guilty of killing his wife, Jack had never gotten accusatory toward him. Jack Johnson had been the classic "good cop" throughout his career.

Jack knocked on Gary's office door. Robbins looked up and motioned him in. Jack explained "I'm picking up some parts for the marina, and had a few minutes to kill, so I decided to stick my head in and say hello." Then he started trying to connect some dots.

He told Gary, "I've been thinking about Mary's disappearance and a few questions occurred to me that I could not recall the answers to. Do you mind talking about it?"

Gary said no, so Jack started asking. "Gary, did you ever found any information about the identity of Mary's friend that she was planning to spend the night with?

Gary responded "No I never found out who she was, I realize now that I didn't really know who any of her friends were."

"How long were the walks that Mary took? "

"They usually took about a ½ hour's time. She would go down to the nude beach at the end of the point and back."

"Did Mary ever stay on the beach for any length of time?"

"No, she preferred to sunbathe on the rear patio at the house. The back yard was fenced in and it afforded her more privacy. Sometimes she liked to sunbathe topless."

"Did Mary ever say anything about the people using the nude beach on the end of the point?"

"Only that most of the sunbathers appeared to be gay or lesbian. Not like us. Mary was never very comfortable with homosexuality."

"Was Mary homophobic?"

"Probably yes, she was at the least extremely uncomfortable around gays because of her upbringing. Her parents were conservative Baptists and Mary carried a lot of baggage stemming from their beliefs."

"How would Mary have reacted if she had been confronted by a gay or a lesbian?"

"Jack, she most likely would have just walked away. She was not really a confrontational person."

"Could Mary have met a friend or neighbor on the beach that day, and gone somewhere with them?"

"Anything is possible. She might even still be alive. After all, no one had ever figured out what happened to her that day, or Mary would not still be missing."

"Do you have any information that would indicate that she was still alive?"

"Unfortunately, I don't have any information like that."

"Do you have any feeling, all these years later, who might have been involved with Mary's disappearance?"

"In hindsight I think she might have been having an affair. I had been running around plenty, so it makes sense to me that perhaps Mary had been also."

"Whom might Mary have had an affair with?"

"It might have been a fellow teacher that she worked with. She was friendly with several of her colleagues. There were also several male students that she tutored that she talked with on the telephone quite regularly, even on weekends.

It was only years later, after a couple of highly publicized affairs between teachers and students, that I considered that possibility. I really don't know with any certainty that she was having an affair."

"Do you remember the names of any of her fellow teachers or of the students who she had tutored?"

"No, but I still have a list of the students somewhere. I've never thrown out her box of school things. I didn't know if I should."

"Could I get a copy of the list from you Gary?"

"Sure Jack, that's not a problem, but why? Is there new evidence about the case?"

"No, Gary there isn't. I was just thinking things over again and wanted to make sure I didn't miss anything. It was my first case as a detective and it's always bothered me that it went unsolved."

Jack had pushed far enough with Gary Robbins. It gave him a few things to look into. A confrontation with a radical gay; an affair with a fellow teacher or student; or that she was still alive somewhere; there were possibilities. Jack would be busy.

The last thing Jack mentioned to Gary was Bennie Richards' death.

 "Gary, I'm surprised that you didn't attend Bennie Richards' wake and service as Bennie's dad had been a good customer of Robbins Auto Parts for years."

Gary replied "I never met Bennie Richards. My dad is living in Florida and did not know about his death. If he had, he undoubtedly would have called me and instructed me to attend and send flowers."

"Thanks for the time Gary, I should go back out front and pick up the parts for my motor."

When Jack left Robbins he drove back downtown to the Photo Garden to pick up his enlargements and went home to his boat. It had been just another day in paradise.

CHAPTER 19

The next morning Jack had to oversee one of his least favorite duties at the marina. The Brendon's Sewage Service truck showed up at 6:30 AM to pump out the holding tank where the human waste from marine toilets on boats was pumped and stored. It was a smelly and dirty job, but someone had to do it and Jack was that someone.

Charlie Smith, the truck driver, loved to gossip whenever he could. One of George Andrews' daughters had married Bob Brendon the founder of the business.

Charlie said that Bob and George's daughter Sarah were on the outs. Bob was the one who currently was running all of George's waste management enterprises. George was threatening to throw Bob out of the business and ruin him. Bob was out for blood from George.

According to Charlie, Bob had been bragging that he knew where all of George's skeletons were hidden and would expose him for the crook that he was if George did not reward Bob generously for having put up with spoiled Sarah for 18 years.

Jack told Charlie that he should stay quiet about such things if he valued his job. Andrews' family affairs easily turned into mini-wars and there was usually extensive collateral damage from them.

Jack could not imagine why people unloaded on him like that. Now he wondered what the real story was. He did not have time or the inclination to follow up on Charlie's story.

Jack had only been half kidding with Charlie about potential collateral damage. It went back to yet another of his father's wisdoms …If you don't have a dog in a fight; leave him on the porch… Jack had no fight with George Andrews.

Jack got to work on the motor rebuild for the Donzi as soon as he finished his daily janitor and dock boy duties at the marina.

He loved working on mechanical things when it was at his own pace. It was a rewarding feeling to turn the key and have something that you assembled from pieces come to life.

If Jack had not become a cop when he got out of the navy, he probably would have gone to tech school and become a mechanic.

Today they were called automotive technicians and he was aware of a few who were making in excess of $70.000 per year in flat rate shops in the area. Not bad for a "grease monkey".

Jack tore down the motor to its basic components. Then he put all the metal parts into a 55 gallon drum filled part way up with kerosene. It would act as a good grease cutter and de-rusting solvent.

After a 24 hour soaking, he would scrub the remaining mess away with a strong brush, and start in the delicate re-assembly of the motor. He should be done in about 2 ½ days. Then he could start on the boat floor.

CHAPTER 20

Memorial Day weekend would be arriving in a few more days. Jack had already launched most of the 108 boats that had been in winter storage at the marina and filled the docks with their summer residents.

The Donzi motor was rebuilt. Because he was so busy launching the boats, he sent Eddie Michaels, one of the young men who helped at the marina during the summer season, down to Lake George to pick up the transmission and propeller shaft assembly. The cushions and seats were reupholstered and ready to install.

Now that the spring rush had passed, tomorrow Jack would be able to pull out the old carpet and floor so he could replace them. If he could stay on schedule, Conrad O'Brien would be able to make the vintage boat parade in the Donzi on July 4th. Without unforeseen problems, he should have time to spare.

Jack finally had the time to follow up with his friend at Vermont DMV, and get the names and current addresses of the three car owners who had been towed from Shelburne Point on the day that Mary Robbins had disappeared. He planned to start talking to them right after the weekend.

He was still not sure what he was looking for. Maybe one of the people he would be talking to would be able to help him connect some dots.

The photo enlargements had shown several sunbathers on the beach, watching as the towing occurred. He hoped some of the car owners could identify a few of the sunbathers and he would have more possible witnesses.

He had gone back to Jean Richards' house a few nights earlier. He had returned the original photos to her, keeping the copies that he had made in a shoebox on his boat.

Terry and the boys had been there, so Jean had prepared cheeseburgers and potato salad for dinner. Jack re-examined Bennie's computer and found nothing that helped any further.

He told Jean that he had gone about as far as he could on Bennie's accident. She reluctantly accepted that the accident was just that, nothing more. He hoped she would come to peace with it. She deserved it.

His gut was still telling him to continue, but he didn't share this feeling with Jean so it wouldn't give her false hope. If he found out more he would share it with her at an appropriate time.

CHAPTER 21

Jack had been too busy to visit with his mother, Myrtle, when he had met her at the Burlington Airport upon her return from Florida for the summer earlier in the week. His brother Tim had been there to take her to his house in Rutland.

Tim had moved back to Rutland when he had graduated from high school in 1973 and gone to work at the General Electric manufacturing plant there. When Newell had died in 1978, he had asked their mother to move back to Rutland and keep house with him, as he had never married.

Now approaching her 87th birthday, she was much sought after by all six of her children. She spent her summers visiting at their various homes for several days at a time.

Jack's home was the exception. A houseboat was not the place for an 87 year old woman to stay, even for a few days. He contented himself with seeing as much as he could of her when she visited his sister Carol's. He decided to call her that evening to see how she was doing.

After catching up on the various health challenges that Jack's aging aunts and uncles were facing, his mother informed him that she would be in Burlington, staying with Carol, for the July 4th weekend and would love to see the fireworks from the water one more time if possible.

Jack told her that he would try to accommodate her, but not to think that it would be her last opportunity, as he was sure that she would live forever.

Myrtle Johnson had always been adventurous. She was the oldest of three children. As a child, she had found a love for learning. There had never been any doubt about her future. She would be a schoolteacher.

After graduating from high school at the age of sixteen, she attended Castleton School for Teaching, which later became Castleton Teachers College. Upon completion of her education, she taught for several years in one room schoolhouses around the Rutland area. Her younger sister Dorothy had also attended Castleton and taught locally.

Myrtle would have never married, except for her sister. Dorothy met and fell in love with Joseph Johnson a local farmer and Newell's brother. Myrtle was maid of honor at their wedding and Newell was best man.

Newell was a confirmed bachelor, and Myrtle was a happy spinster when they met. Dorothy and Joseph decided that their sister and brother should experience the same joy that they felt. They worked tirelessly to match them up. They succeeded in 1940 when the two started to date.

Newell was drafted into the Army Air Corp for World War II. He and Myrtle shared a long distance romance for 4 ½ years until he was discharged and they were married.

Newell went to work for the Goldstein family as bookkeeper at the Bardwell and Berwick hotels in Rutland, starting his career in the hospitality business.

He insisted that Myrtle stay at home to take care of their children. She happily agreed and spent the next 36 years as a full time mother to six. When Jack's father had died in 1978, Myrtle went back to her first love.

She spent several years working with special needs children in Rutland before retiring so that she could winter in Florida. During those years, she learned to swim and ride a bicycle.

One of Jack's favorite pictures was of Myrtle at age 85 riding her bicycle. It had been on the front page of the Rutland Herald along with a wonderful story about her poetry.

She went each Monday during the summer to a nursing home in Rutland so that she could read to the "old people" who lived there. She had just had her first book of poetry published.

During Jack's marriage to Sally, Myrtle had gone sailing with them several times, including one July 4th weekend fifteen years earlier. She had exclaimed then that the only way to really enjoy the annual Burlington fireworks display was from the water.

She had even compared it to the experience that Francis Scott Key had witnessed in Baltimore harbor during the war of 1812, inspiring him to write the Star Spangled Banner.

Jack had promised that if the weather cooperated that he would take her and his sister out on the broad lake to enjoy the spectacle this year.

He might even try to get all of his siblings and their children to go. Sixteen Johnson's would be a crowd on the boat, but his mother would cherish the memory.

CHAPTER 22

There was nothing more effective in producing a slow day at a marina than a cold drizzle with gusty winds. That was how the day was stacking up at Marble Island.

After doing his normal routine of cleaning and checking the boats in their slips Jack went to the boat shed to tackle replacing the floor and carpet on the Donzi. First, he tore out the old carpet.

Next he attacked the screws that held in floorboards. He was able to remove a few with a screwdriver most had to be drilled out due to rust and corrosion.

Most of the old floor back at the stern was deeply stained with rust. It was otherwise in much better condition than he had anticipated.

He wondered in passing what had been placed on the floor that had caused the stain. It must have been something metallic that had been left sitting on the boat for quite awhile.

John Patch

He made good progress. Because the old floor was sturdier than he had expected he removed it carefully and used it for a precise pattern for the replacement.

After he had cut out the new floor panels and before he started to install them, he tackled re-installing the rebuilt power train. It was a much easier job without having to work around the tight opening in the floor.

By mid-afternoon, Jack had the motor, transmission and propeller shaft securely re-installed. He decided to put off the installation of the new floor until the next morning when he was fresh. He could spend the next few hours on the phone trying to contact the owners of the cars that had been towed from Shelburne Point.

His first call was to Jim Caldwell, a local insurance agent who had been a college student in 1978. Jim vaguely remembered having his car towed.

Caldwell had been around the corner at the end of the point on the nude beach with a friend for the afternoon and did not find out that his car had been towed until he walked back around the point and discovered it missing at dinnertime.

Jack asked if he remembered any disturbance involving a single woman or a couple that might have occurred during the late morning or early afternoon. Jim did not recall any other details of the day except his car being towed. An incident on the beach would have stuck in his mind. Strike one!

His next call was to Jane Trono at a Shelburne address. She remembered the day quite clearly. She was at the beach with her two young children, and had argued with the police and tow truck operator about the legality of towing her car.

She ended up having to write a check for the tow operator even though he didn't actually tow her car. She had interrupted him just after he had hooked it up to his sling.

She also received a ticket from the police for illegal parking. She was quite angry and left with her kids immediately.

It had spoiled her youngest son's 4th birthday. She had barely had time to snap a few pictures of the kids on the beach and unpack her picnic basket when she saw her car hooked up to the tow truck.

They had ended up driving into Burlington and going to North Beach to finish their birthday celebration. She did not remember any single woman walking on the beach while she was there. Strike two!

His last call was to Jacob Dowe. Jacob was a business department professor at UVM nearing retirement. He told Jack that his daughter Gretchen had been there with his wife's car that day.

He had to cancel a business appointment so that he could pick them up and drive them into Burlington to retrieve the car at the end of the day. He had taken away her car privileges for a month.

She had been in high school and had no exams scheduled that day. She and a few of her friends had decided to go to the beach and get an early start on their tans.

She was married now with three children. Her married name was Miller and she and her husband lived in Boston Massachusetts.

Jack got Gretchen's telephone number from Jacob and tried to reach her. He got an answering machine and left his name, number and a brief message explaining his interest in her memories of the day. He hoped she would return his call.

It occurred to Jack that the pictures that Jane Trono had taken might show something that she did not remember. He called her back and asked if she still had them.

She said they were in an old photo album. She would get them out and Jack could look at them if he wanted.

He did, so he drove down to Shelburne to look at some pictures. He took the three enlargements that he had from Bennie's collection to show her.

He was hoping she might identify someone in his photos so he would have more people to talk to about that day.

Jack found the Trono house in Juniper Ridge just off from Shelburne Road. Jane and her husband had bought their raised ranch newly built in 1976.

They had raised their two sons there and were now approaching retirement. She had coffee and cookies prepared when he knocked on the door.

CHAPTER 23

Before Jack could start asking any more questions of Jane Trono, she required him to answer a few for her. He explained that the Mary Robbins disappearance had been his first case as a police detective.

He stuck with the story that he had used with Gary Robbins about wanting to be sure in his own mind that he had not missed anything that might solve the case.

When Jane was satisfied regarding Jack's motive, she got out her old photo album with the pictures from May 23, 1978.

Jack noticed that several of the people from Ritchie's photos were also in Jane's. He asked, "Mrs. Trono, do you recognize anyone else in the pictures other than your children?"

She pointed to a young woman. She was with the owner of one of the other cars that was towed that day. There were several high school girls that were there together. I remember that the owner was out in the water wind surfing.

This girl tried to catch her attention so she could move the car before it was towed."

Jack assumed that the wind surfer was Gretchen Miller and this was one of her girlfriends who went to the beach with her.

Jane also pointed to an older woman. "Her name is Leanne Wilson. She lived in the development across the street. It was she who had called the police to have the cars towed. She went up and down the beach telling all of the people that they were trespassing on private property and would have to leave or be arrested."

"Even the police officer who was overseeing the towing operation seemed to dislike her snotty attitude as she paraded around yelling at everyone. He asked her several times to return to her home and let him do his job."

It did not seem like much, but Jack left with more information than he arrived with. He recalled the name Leanne Wilson from somewhere.

He would look into it and hopefully find out more. He thanked Jane Trono for her help and headed back to Marble Island.

Jack's cell phone rang as he was pulling into the marina parking lot. It was Gretchen Miller returning his call from earlier that day. He asked her if she remembered the day that her mother's car was towed from Shelburne Point Beach?

She replied, "I remember that day because of two things. First, I was nearly run over on the lake off from the tip of Shelburne Point while I was wind surfing by a couple of kids in a speedboat."

"When I got back onto shore there was some crazy woman yelling at everyone about trespassing on private property, and the police had had my mother's car towed."

"I had to call my father and confess. He was so upset that he grounded me and took away my car privileges for half the summer."

"Overall, it turned out to be not the fun day that my girl friends and I had anticipated when we decided to spend the day at the beach."

Jack's next question was "Do you remember having seen Mary Robbins on the beach that day?"

"I was one of Mary Robbins high school English students. I remember that she disappeared that around that time. I never thought about the fact that it was the day I was at the beach."

"I can't be sure but I think that I saw Mary walking on the path to the point near the Shipyard while I was rigging up my sailboard that day."

"I never considered that having possibly seen her walking on the path had any significance regarding her disappearance. I figured it was Mary's asshole husband who was responsible for her disappearance."

"He had the nerve to come on to me at Al's French Fries one night a few months before the disappearance when I was there with a few of my girl friends."

"He was there eating with a couple of his friends. He was too old, too loud, and too drunk for me or any of my friends. He hadn't even bothered to take off his wedding band. One of my friends knew who he was and identified him as Mary Robbins' husband."

"I followed the story of her disappearance in the newspaper, like almost everyone else. I was convinced that her jerky husband must have been behind it."

"I'll be coming to Burlington with my kids to visit my parents when school gets out in June. It's only a couple of weeks away. I'll ask my girl friends if any of them remember anything else from that day."

"We're planning to get together for a reunion to catch up with each other. If anyone remembers anything, I can call you and let you know."

Jack got Gretchen's Boston address from her so he could send her a copy of the beach pictures to see if she could identify anyone.

She said she would return them to her father's house when she visited. He thanked her and hung up.

He went to his boat, lit a cigar and sat with a cold beer enjoying the sunset. His gut told him that there was something out there, and he was on his way to finding out what it was.

CHAPTER 24

It was Friday morning, the calm before the storm. Memorial Day weekend started with sunshine and a light southerly breeze. That afternoon would bring the true start to the boating season.

Jack made his rounds of the marina, making sure that the vending machines, especially the one dispensing ice were all full and working properly.

When he had finished checking things on and around the docks, Jack went to the boat shed to work on the Donzi. He installed the new floorboards and laid down the new carpet.

He then cleaned up the mess he had made around the boat, piling the old floorboards in the corner, and tossing the old carpet on top of them.

He barely had time to finish cleaning up before the first dock accident of the season occurred. Kenneth "Captain Crunch" Paquette, a new boater at the marina had run into two boats docked opposite his when he tried to leave the marina for a ride around the bay.

Paquette was a trucker who did a lot of hauling for George Andrews' distribution business. Without that business, he would more than likely be working for a moving company.

Fortunately, little property damage was done. He would have to move "Captain Crunch" to an outer dock slip so he would not repeat the docking mishap.

Nick Griffith, the manager at Mills Point Marina had mentioned Paquette's nickname to Jack when he had gone over with the marina trailer to transport his boat, which had previously been docked with Nick.

Captain Crunch had apparently learned little from the boating safety course he had been required to complete as the result of an accident in the bay the previous season.

As Newell Johnson had told Jack many times … you can lead a horse to water, but you can't make him drink…

There were many boaters on the lake besides Paquette who really were not experienced enough to safely operate their vessels.

It made little sense to Jack that the law required that a person needed to pass a test and obtain a license to operate a motor vehicle, or pilot an airplane, but not to operate a boat.

CHAPTER 25

Things continued to be busy at the marina throughout the long weekend. Jack and his two assistants were kept on their toes by the boaters comings and goings.

It was Monday afternoon before there was finally a lull as people left the marina to return to their homes for the work week.

Jack was on the docks checking lines and electrical/water hook ups when he looked up and saw Louis O'Brien walking toward him. He could not remember ever seeing Louis on the docks before.

Louis and Martha had built their cottage on the west side of Marble Island facing Thayer's Bay so they could enjoy the sunsets over the Adirondack Mountains.

They had their own dock and moorings in the cove in front of their cottage, so they never used the marina facilities. Even as a young man, Louis had never come around the resort.

His father had been something of an embarrassment to the rest of the O'Brien family, so there was never much interaction with his Uncle Charles or his family, who had lived on the Marble Island each summer.

Louis III's brood lived in Burlington year round and only occasionally used the family cottage located on the north cove on Pebble Beach during the summer seasons.

Jack had always felt that Louis IV and Conrad acted more like fighting brothers than cousins. He had certainly never seen much friendliness exhibited between them, only sibling rivalry.

… You can choose your friends, but you can't choose your relatives… came to mind. It was another of Newell Johnson's pearls of wisdom.

Louis said, "Jack, I just learned that you're rebuilding the old Donzi that Conrad and I shared as teenagers. What kind of shape it was in after so many years in storage? Could I have a look at the project?"

Jack answered "Certainly you can Louis. I'll be happy to give you the nickel tour of the progress I've made so far."

They went to the shed and Jack pulled off the tarp to exhibit the progress with the restoration. He and Louis discussed the amount of work that had been needed.

Jack went into quite a bit of detail about the motor rebuild, the poor state of the upholstery and carpet, the fortunate fact that it was a fiberglass hull, and the surprisingly good condition of the floor boards after almost 30 years.

After the inspection of the boat, Louis offered Jack an expensive Ashley cigar. He accepted it quickly, and offered Louis a cold beer on his boat.

They went back down the docks and boarded. Jack got a Sam Adams for Louis and an Excel for himself. They settled into two canvas chairs on the foredeck and relaxed with their cigars.

Louis started talking. "That Donzi was a very big part of my youth. It was always hard sharing the boat with my cousin. Conrad always had first dibs on its use, and would never clean it up after he had used it."

"I spent nearly as much time maintaining the appearance of the boat as I did using it on the lake. The fuel tank was always empty when it was my turn to use it, and I continually had to replace lost or broken water skis."

"One time Conrad had even lost the anchor and rode. I'm happy to see that it's being restored now. I probably never would have married Martha without the boat. I used it firstly to impress her with my fabulous water skiing abilities in front of her grandparent's camp on Shelburne Point. Later we used to escape from her grandparents and my cousin."

"Martha and I spent many a summer day alone out on the lake sharing their hopes and aspirations. We fell in love on board the boat."

Jack asked "Why didn't you buy the boat from Conrad when your Uncle Charles died if it meant so much to you?"

"Thirteen years ago I was immersed in my new law practice and my young family. Buying another boat was very low on my list of priorities at that point in my life."

"A few months ago, Bennie Richards had asked me if I knew what had become of it when I stopped by his mini mart to pick up some milk on my way home from City Hall."

"I had lost track of the boat when I went away to college, and had assumed that it had been sold and I told Bennie that."

"Bennie told me that the Donzi was stored in the boat shed at Marble Island and thought it might still belong to me. That got me thinking about the Donzi and my youth. The more I thought about it the more I realized the part it had played in my courtship and marriage to Martha. I just found out that it's being restored."

"I asked Conrad what had become of it. I feigned not having any knowledge of it's being here thinking that I could buy it from him cheap."

"Conrad told me that he was having it restored for his fiancé. I knew that if I showed much interest in it that Conrad would ask a lot more for the boat."

"As soon as Conrad and his fiancé find out that the Donzi is too small and too slow for their tastes I should be able to buy it from him for less than the cost of the restoration."

"Jack, I want you to let me know when that happens so I can act on it. I'm certain that Martha would appreciate the Donzi as a twenty fifth anniversary gift this October. I'm confident Conrad will be tired of the novelty of an old boat by then."

After they finished their cigars and Louis left, Jack realized that their conversation was the first time that he had ever seen Louis let his guard down. He had seen Louis's feelings of insecurity within his family, his love for Martha and his compassion for the memories of the Donzi. It had obviously been an important part of his past.

Apparently, Louis O'Brien IV was a real human being after all, not just a political animal who used people to achieve his personal goals and feed his own ego.

That might even explain why he had shown up at Bennie Richards' service. Perhaps Louis was a lot more like his Uncle Charles than Jack had realized.

CHAPTER 26

Tuesday morning at 8:00 AM brought a telephone call from Joe Andrews. He wanted to give Jack a heads up. Bennie Richards' insurance company had called to find out the recovery and storage costs for his van.

The police had released it, and the insurance company was picking it up tomorrow. Jack thanked him and hung up.

He drove into Burlington to Richards Mini Mart and had Jean write a note authorizing him to pick up the personal items from the van. He told her that he would drop them off to her sometime soon.

He then went to Andrews Salvage and gave the note to Joe to pass on to the insurance company for their records.

Jack took his old 35mm camera with him to the yard. After he had taken several pictures of the exterior and interior of the van, he gathered up the contents of the glove compartment as well as the coffee mug, soda can, and cigarette packs from the interior and placed them in plastic bags.

It was an old habit that he had learned when he had been handling evidence at crime scenes. He then took off the license plates and left, thanking Joe again for the heads up.

Jack was not certain that there was anything important in what he did. It was more of a feeling than anything else. He only knew that once the van was removed it would be crushed and recycled. There would be no revisiting it after that had occurred.

Jack returned to Marble Island and took the plastic bags with Bennie's belongings from the wrecked van to his boat.

He placed them in the shoebox with his copies of Bennie's photos. That way everything was in one place.

Jack went back to work on the Donzi. Today he would start work on cleaning up the hull. He removed the windshield and deck hardware. He then taped off the waterline and interior so he could use a power buffer on the topsides.

It was slow work but very rewarding, using the buffer first with rubbing compound to restore the colors, and then waxing the finish to a high luster to complete the job.

When he had finished for the day at 7:00 P.M., before he closed up the shed for the night, he stripped off the masking tape and washed down the dust from the concrete floor. He stood back to admire his progress.

It was easy to see why Donzi Boats were still so popular even today. The white hull with yellow striping had returned to life in its former splendor. The lines were clean and classic looking.

Tomorrow he would re-install the windshield and deck hardware. Then all that would be left to do was to apply the anti-fouling bottom paint and install the new seats and interior trim. He was anxious to get the boat in the water and try it out.

Only after he worked out the bugs would he inform Conrad that it was seaworthy. Jack just hoped that he would appreciate the vessel as much as his cousin Louis would.

Or he would at least sell it to Louis after he and his fiancé participated in the July 4th vintage boat parade on Burlington's waterfront.

CHAPTER 27

Jack woke up on Wednesday morning feeling as if he had never slept the previous night. He had tossed and turned endlessly before finally dozing off early in the morning.

Then he dreamt of the photos that Bennie Richards had taken on Shelburne Point the day of Mary Robbins disappearance. He could not shake the feeling that there was something there that he was missing.

His morning routine of cleaning the bathrooms, dumping the trash, filling the vending machines and checking the docks was completed by 10 A.M.

He needed to purchase the Bottom-Kote paint for the Donzi, so he told Eddy Michaels, one of the part time dock boys that he would be gone for a half hour. He drove to Lakeshore Hardware and Marine to purchase the paint and some cleaning solvent.

While Jack was at the store, he ran into Nick Griffith, the manager of the Mills Point Marina. He told Nick about the Captain Crunch dock incident that had occurred.

Nick told him that he was not surprised in the least. Paquette was bad news as far as he was concerned. He was glad to see him go. It was too bad he had ended up at Marble Island.

He was sorry he had not thought to warn Jack. He had just been happy when Paquette had decided to leave his marina.

Nick and Jack had graduated from Burlington High School together. They had been in the several of the same classes throughout high school.

Nick had started working as a dock boy at Shelburne Shipyard summers while in high school. He loved being around boats, and ended up going full time after graduation.

He had an incredible memory for the boat owners' names. Well liked, proficient, and polite, within a few years he was promoted to manager. A position he held onto for twenty years.

Nick had always been a hard drinker. When his marriage went bad, he started sneaking nips from a bottle that he kept hidden at work. When he dropped a 38 foot sailboat from the slings while launching it, he found himself without a job.

He bounced around for a couple of years working for a boat broker and sinking further into the bottle.

The job at Mills Point Marina opened up when the owners found out that the manager who was Nick's predecessor had been embezzling from them.

Nick had recently dried out had been given the job with the condition that he not start drinking again. Three years later, he was still at it.

The owners were hands off, allowing Nick to do things his way. Knowing that this was his last chance on Lake Champlain, he buckled down and was doing a great job.

Nick asked Jack what he was working on. Jack told him the O'Brien's Donzi. Nick recalled the tension between the two cousins when they were kids and shared the use of it.

He laughed about one incident in particular when Conrad had pushed his cousin off the dock and took off with the boat before Louis could climb back out of the lake.

He was a little put off to think that Conrad owned it now. Nick thought the boat deserved better. Jack told him to call or stop by sometime and went back to Marble Island to work on the boat.

CHAPTER 28

Jack drove back to the marina and spent the rest of the day applying the anti-fouling paint to the hull of the Donzi. He finished early enough so he was able to reinstall the windshield, seats, and upholstery trim. Tomorrow he planned to launch it and give it a test drive in Malletts Bay.

After dinner, he pulled out the box with Bennie's things and started going over the photos again. He ended up concentrating on the enlargements of the pictures from May 23, 1978, the day of Mary Robbins disappearance and assumed murder. He didn't spot anything about the cars or people in the photos that seemed noteworthy.

After scrutinizing everything for several minutes Jack started to put them away when he noticed what might have been a boat in the background of the picture Bennie had written his question on the back of. He could not make out the details but there definitely was something in the background of that shot.

He would have to visit the photo lab to see if they could blow the picture up some more and sharpen the details before he could determine what, if any, significance it would disclose... Patience was a virtue... Newell had always proclaimed. Jack would just have to be patient.

Just as he was falling asleep, Jack's cell phone rang. It was Gary Robbins. From the slurring in his speech, it was apparent that he had had quite a few drinks.

Robbins started decrying the injustice of the stigma he had been living under since Mary's disappearance, stating again his innocence. Then he sobbingly proclaimed how much they had loved each other.

After composing himself somewhat he went into great detail of how this terrible injustice had hurt his standing in the community for all of these years.

He said he just wanted to tell Jack how much he appreciated his looking into the incident again. He was certain that something would turn up exonerating him.

He finished after about 20 minutes by saying that he hoped that Jack would earn the $50,000 reward that was still being offered by his family for the true events that had led to Mary's disappearance.

After Robbins finally hung up Jack knew that he would not be sleeping well tonight. His interest was not in Gary Robbins life, and he found it uncomfortable to have him, or anyone else thinking that.

It was Bennie Richards' death. Anything more was unimportant to him. This was not a labor for monetary gain. It was something he needed to do for Bennie's family, for his own father's memory, and for himself, nothing more.

CHAPTER 29

Thursday morning Jack performed his routine at the marina quickly. When he finished he hooked up the Donzi and trailer to the back of his truck and drove off the island to the state boat access ramp.

He did not want Conrad O'Brien to see the boat in the water until he was satisfied that everything was in good working order. The last thing he needed would be for his employer to have a breakdown on the lake in the restored Donzi.

He launched the boat, walked it over and tied it off to the launch dock, and pulled his truck and trailer into the parking lot.

When he boarded and turned the key, the small block Ford motor started immediately and idled smoothly. He cast off the dock and slowly pulled out of the cove into the outer bay beyond the no wake zone.

The boat's response as he opened the throttle was gratifying. It quickly went up on plane and cut through the light chop smoothly. This was what life was about thought Jack.

Open water, a powerful boat, sunny weather and a clear course ahead to the open lake.

He decided to go down to Burlington and have a coffee at Breakers. It would be a 34 mile round trip. Any kinks should show up on a cruise of that length.

When twenty five minutes after leaving the access area he pulled up to the customer dock at Breakers in Burlington, Tony Kravits, whose father owned the Lake Champlain Ferry Service located on the quay just behind and next to the restaurant, was standing on the dock to catch his lines for him.

Almost before Jack could climb off the boat, Tony was all over it. He asked Jack where he had found such a beautiful Donzi.

Tony said that he had wanted one since he was a little kid and had watched the O'Brien boys waterskiing with theirs back in the 1970's.

Jack told him that it was the same boat and still belonged to Conrad. Tony was surprised, as he had approached Conrad several years ago to see if he could buy it. Conrad had told Tony that it had been sold to an out of state buyer soon after Charles' death.

They sat down with two coffees and Jack told Tony about all of the work that he had performed on the boat to bring it back to life. Tony asked Jack if he would be willing to do a similar restoration for him if he came up with a boat.

Jack told him to find his dream boat and as long as it was made of fiberglass and the hull was sound that he would enjoy such a project.

All it would take is money. Tony said he would be in touch and walked back to the ferry offices to go to work.

Jack sat at Breakers for a few more minutes before boarding and casting off to return to Malletts Bay. The return trip went as smoothly as the cruise down.

He decided that rather than going back to the boat access, he would leave the Donzi in a slip at the docks at Marble Island Marina and parked it there.

As he walked to the marina office, he looked back and admired the way that the boat sat in the water.

He had Eddie drop him off at the boat access so that he could pick up his truck and return the boat trailer to the shed at the marina. When he finished with that he went to his boat and picked up the photo that he needed worked on.

Jack drove to downtown Burlington and went into the Photo Garden to talk with them about enlarging and enhancing the image in the background of the picture.

The owner of the Photo Garden looked at the print, discussed what Jack wanted to do, and suggested that he send it to an out of state photo lab that had more sophisticated developing equipment and would be more likely to achieve the results Jack was hoping for.

First, they would make a new negative from the original photo. It would take a few days for the out of state lab to do the work and ship it back to Burlington. He should have it back by next Wednesday.

In the meantime, Jack would do some more checking on events that had happened in Shelburne with Leanne Wilson, the bitchy neighborhood lady who had been on the beach. He had finally recalled why her name had been familiar.

She was an active member of the Conservation Law Organization, and had been at the forefront of an attempt in the early 1990's to put marinas on the lake out of business by claiming that their docks violated the public trust doctrine.

This woman was the epitome of hypocrisy. On one hand, she had fought to prohibit access to "her lakeshore" on Shelburne Point, and on the other, she was attacking the marina industry for inhibiting peoples free access to the lake. Perhaps she should be listed in the dictionary under oxymoron.

Jack had given her a call and she agreed to meet with him at her husband's office in Williston. Her husband was a chiropractor and she was the office manager.

He doubted that she would be able to add anything to what she had remembered during her initial interview about anything that had happened on the beach the day of Mary Robbins disappearance.

She could however share some information about Mary and Gary's comings and goings to their home. She was a nosy neighbor who he was sure would have made it her business to try to know theirs.

Jack ended up spending two hours with Wilson, and learned more than he had wanted to know about the development on the point.

She had listed all of the homeowners who had violated various covenants, how much money they made, which couples got along, whose kids had smoking pot, etc… etc…

She and her chiropractor had moved on in the early 1980's to a bigger home with lake access closer to the Charlotte town line. When the property they crossed to reach the lake access was sold, the new owner had closed off their access.

They had not bothered to record their access agreement that they had made with the old owner of the property in the town offices. Consequently, they now had none.

She went into detail explaining the Conservation Law Organization's interpretation of the Public Trust Doctrine.

The original Doctrine was limited to Railroads right of ways over public property. In the 1970's the city of Burlington had successfully challenged the Central Vermont Railways ownership of a large part of the old Burlington waterfront that was no longer in use as a rail yard.

The only thing left from the rail operation was some decrepit unused sidings. The courts had ruled that ownership would revert to Burlington in exchange for a minimal payment to the Railroad.

From that ruling, the Conservation Law Organization decided to attempt a new precedent similar to the one that the state of Maine had achieved in the 1960's.

Private ownership of the Maine coastline was prohibited between the high and low watermarks of the coast.

Furthermore, public access to the public lands must be maintained.

The Conservation Law Organization argued that the same should be true for Lake Champlain lakeshore, and sought to have all of the lakes shoreline between 95.5 feet above sea level, the established mean low water mark used on lake charts, and the 100.5 foot level, the established flood stage of the lake be recognized as belonging to the public. Access to the publicly owned strip of land should not be restricted by private landowners

That explained why Wilson's perspective on lake access had changed. It was simply sour grapes over her personal situation.

She had also been able to recall with great detail the actions of the Robbins couple when they had been neighbors. She had seen Gary bring home young bimbos while Mary was at work a more than a few times, and had made it her business to tell Mary about it.

Mary's reaction had been sadness, not anger Wilson said. It was as if she had already known and come to terms with his infidelity. She also remembered that Mary had a girlfriend who visited her quite often.

She thought her name was Vicky something. She had been there for dinner the day before Mary had disappeared. Leanne had heard her say to Mary as she was leaving that she would see her the next evening.

She had tried to tell a Shelburne patrol officer about it at the time. The patrol officer had told her that a detective might be in touch but no one had ever contacted her about it.

She had not talked about it again with anyone else because the police had treated her poorly over the parking situation in front of the beach that had belonged to the development.

Jack needed to talk to Mary Robbins known friends to see if any of them knew who Vicky was.

Maybe Mary really had been planning on spending that night at a girl friends place. The mysterious Vicky might have helped her escape her marriage. Perhaps Gary Robbins final version of events was not all smoke after all.

If that were the case, why wouldn't Mary have come forward since? She certainly had no reason to have changed her identity permanently and abandoned her family.

No one that Jack had ever heard of would go that far to hurt their spouse when it would also cause such anguish to her friends and family, and he had met many vindictive people in his life.

If Vicky had been a friend of Mary's and known anything that would help in the investigation, why wouldn't she have come forward at the time? Were the two of them lovers? Had they disappeared together? Were they both dead? Was her friend responsible for Mary's disappearance or death? New questions abounded.

Now it was up to Jack to try to find some new answers. First, he had to take care of his responsibilities at the Marina this weekend. Newell Johnson's son could do nothing less.

CHAPTER 30

The weekend was warm and sunny. That made for a lot of traffic at the marina, which meant that Jack was on 24 hour duty.

Late on Friday night Kenneth Paquette caused another disturbance on the docks. He had been partying with his wife and another couple since early evening.

Apparently, after the other couple had gone home, Paquette and his wife had a disagreement about whether or not to stay on board overnight.

It had ended up with him smacking his wife around when she insisted that she was not staying on the boat when he was drunk and ornery. Another boater had run to Jack's boat to summon him.

Jack had to pull Paquette off his wife, and then escorted her to a cab so she could go home. He had called the Colchester Police and they had arrested Paquette, taking him away in handcuffs.

The idiot had taken a swing at one of the cops, so he ended up going to the correctional center for the rest of the weekend.

He would be arraigned on Monday morning for spousal abuse, and assaulting a police officer.

Jack decided that Captain Crunch would have to be moving his boat again, as he had violated his boater lease agreement.

He would be expelled from Marble Island immediately. Jack would do his best to make sure that Paquette's new address would not be in Malletts Bay.

He would call the other Marinas in the bay and let the operators know about the incident. The first thing he did on Saturday morning was to pull Paquette's boat and put it on its cradle in the storage yard.

At eleven in the morning Conrad showed up to see him. He had heard about the previous night's disturbance while having breakfast this morning at the Bayside Bakery, a little restaurant just down Lakeshore Drive from the island road.

It was a local gathering place for residents of the bay. The regulars exchanged gossip each morning over coffee and fresh pastries prepared by the owner.

Conrad had heard a much-exaggerated account of the incident. According to the growing speculation, several boat owners had been involved, and Paquette's wife had been taken to the hospital with serious injuries.

After Jack relayed the true occurrences, he and Conrad had a good laugh over the way that the story had grown so distorted in just a few hours.

Jack decided that it was as good a time as any to show Conrad the Donzi. He took the keys from the marina office and they walked down the docks to the slip where he had placed it the previous day.

Conrad climbed on board and sat at the helm. He started the motor, let it idle for a few minutes and then shut it off and disembarked.

He handed Jack back the keys and asked him to pull it and put it back in the shed until the 4th of July so his fiancé would not see it on the docks.

He seemed angry that it had been left in the water. Jack said he would take care of it right away.

As they walked back to the marina office Jack mentioned running into Tony Kravitz at Breakers the previous day and that he had greatly admired the Donzi and had made it clear how much he would like to own it.

Conrad replied that he would burn the boat before allowing Kravitz to possess it. He said that Kravitz was nothing more than a spoiled kid who would have nothing if it had not been for his father's success and left

….The pot was calling the kettle black…. It was another of his father's little idioms and immediately came to Jack's mind. He found Eddie Michaels and had him take the truck and trailer over to the boat launch.

Jack went back down the docks and cast off in the Donzi so he could meet Eddie and pull the boat. They brought it back, backed it into the shed, and covered it.

He realized that Conrad had not said whether he liked the restoration or not. It was a shame that a boat as beautiful as the Donzi was kept hidden away instead of on the water where it was designed to be.

It was almost as if he did not want to see the boat, just to possess it. He wondered if Conrad would allow even his cousin Louis to buy it from him. He hoped so. It would be a crime to have it stay in storage for another twelve or thirteen years. It would need another restoration if that happened.

The rest of the weekend passed with no more problems at the marina. Most of the boaters were worn out by Sunday noon. Jack's brother Tom showed up on his boat and Jack took the afternoon off to go fishing with him. He left Eddie Michaels in charge and told him that if anything came up he was only a cell call away.

CHAPTER 31

On Monday morning, Jack went quickly about his marina routine. It was time to pump the sewage holding tank again and Charlie Smith showed up late in the morning to do the dirty deed.

Charlie was as gossipy as usual. He caught Jack up on the war between Bob Brendon and his father in law George Andrews.

Things were escalating; Bob had brought in a lawyer and was threatening to sue George if he did not sign over the entire waste management business enterprise to him.

Bob had owned the septic business prior to his marriage to George's daughter. George had merged it in with his trash collection company and made Bob the boss.

Bob figured that he had run it for 18 years, so it should all be his. This could make for a very interesting court battle.

Jack did not think that Bob really had a legal claim on the trash collection end of it, but George was not well liked by some in Burlington so a jury trial would be a gamble. Time would tell.

Jack warned Charlie again about talking out of school. It could end up hurting him if either Bob or George felt he was taking the others side. Charlie had a wife and daughter to take care of, and good paying jobs were not so plentiful right now.

Gretchen Miller called Jack's cell phone at 2:00 P.M. She had arrived in Burlington on Saturday with her two kids.

They were staying at her parents' house for the week. Sunday she had gotten together with her girlfriends and looked at the photos Jack had sent her. They did not recognize any people other than each other in the pictures.

One of her girl friends was certain that she had seen Mary Robbins on the path over near the marina that day. She had walked over to use the boater's bathrooms at lunchtime.

Mary had already passed the gate to the marina and was heading toward the end of the point on the path.

She had not thought anything of it at the time because of the newspaper stories implicating Gary Robbins. Her name was Christy Sullivan. She had married a guy who was employed at Vermont Railway. Christy had kept her maiden name.

Christy was the proprietor of Sully's Bar and Grill in the old Hotel Vermont building. Her father had started the business in the 1950's. Sully's was one of the more popular eating establishments' downtown specializing in steaks and seafood.

If Jack wanted to talk to her, he should stop by between lunch and dinnertime. Her husband was a bit insecure about their marriage, so seeing her away from work would not be a good idea.

Jack planned to stop by Sully's for a chat with Christy the next afternoon. He would try to flush out her memory of seeing Mary Robbins to see if she could recall any additional details.

He arranged with Gretchen to pick up the photos at her parents' house on Tuesday late in the morning and thanked her for her help.

CHAPTER 32

Jack picked up some ground beef and baby red potatoes at Mazza's Store in the bay and called his sister to invite her to dinner at the marina. Mazza's was famous for its ground beef that …melts in your mouth, not in your pan…

Jack however never cooked it any other way than on the grill with pepper jack cheddar cheese and roasted baby reds that he had marinated in olive oil and sea salt. It was a favorite of Carol's.

It had been a few weeks since he had seen her and he felt like bouncing off his findings and feelings about Bennie Richards' death and where it was apparently leading. She was always a good listener, and usually offered some good insights.

When tied up at the docks no boaters were allowed to cook on an open flame as it created a very real fire hazard. The marina provided several gas and charcoal grills on shore.

They were located under a large tent shaped canopy. There were picnic tables for those who chose not to carry their meals back to their boats.

When Carol arrived, she stayed on board with a glass of wine while Jacked grilled their dinner. She was considering early retirement and had brought the information regarding the benefits that were being offered in the latest package that the federal court was offering older employees who had been working for more than twenty-five years.

While they ate, she discussed the pros and cons of taking advantage of the offer. The package was tempting, but she was not sure what she would do with her time, as she did not feel ready to stop working yet.

Maybe she could work at the marina she joked. She could pump fuel in boats wearing a revealing bathing suit. That would be sure to increase business.

Jack said he was not so sure that there were enough horny old goat boat owners on the lake that it would work. Carol splashed a little of her wine at him in response. He decided to change the subject to the Richards investigation.

What had started out as a favor for Joan Richards was turning into an investigation of an unsolved 27 year old suspected murder. Jack still was not sure yet how it all tied together.

"It's starting to look like it may not have been Gary Robbins who was responsible after all. But I'm having a hard time believing that Bennie would not have gone to the authorities so he could claim the reward offered for information if he had found something that solved the case."

Carol thought about it for a few minutes. She asked Jack, "How much you would be willing to pay if you had committed a murder and someone approached you offering to destroy the evidence they had found and remain silent about what they knew?"

Jack replied, "I wouldn't pay him a thing. He would just come back repeatedly sucking more money until there was none left to get."

"Then they would more than likely end up going to the authorities anyway so they could get the reward. The only way to insure his silence would be to kill him."

"Bennie might not have seen things the same way that you do Jack. Perhaps he thought that his information would protect him from harm and it could be worth a lot more than $50,000 if he sold it to the killer."

"If the killer's thought process was the same as yours, there was probably no better way to eliminate Bennie than to stage an accident."

"Now the only thing you need to do to solve the Mary Robbins disappearance/murder case, if your gut is right, is to figure out who arranged Bennie's accident. Then you'd have the guilty party in the Robbins disappearance as well."

Carol had really made the whole situation seem simple. Jack decided to return the conversation to her retirement offer.

He needed a brain break before trying to go further into the disappearance without more information.

Right now, all he had was a gut feeling, and that was not going to solve anything. She left for home just after sunset.

Jack went back over all of the pieces of information and found precious little that amounted to a breakthrough.

He had now verified that Mary Robbins had gone for a walk on the path to Shelburne Point from the edge of her development around the time of her disappearance.

He had learned that she had been told by a neighbor that her husband had been bringing other young women to her home when she was not there. It appeared that this revelation had not surprised her.

No one had seen her after she had taken her walk or return home from it. She had not been seen at the end of the point.

She had a friend named Vicky that no one knew much about. It was overheard that she was supposed to go to Vicky's on the night of her disappearance.

She may have disappeared during her walk not sometime during the night, as everyone had previously believed.

On the other hand, there was no real evidence that she did not return home after her walk. What Jack really needed was to find out if she had or not.

If she had, then Gary Robbins was still the prime suspect. If not then there was no known suspect. He needed to find anyone who had seen her since Christy had.

He needed to talk to Christy and see if she could connect some dots for him. He then needed to find Vicky or whoever she was and see what if anything she could add to the puzzle.

He would start with Christy the next afternoon. Hopefully, she would have some information that would help him get pointed in the right direction.

CHAPTER 33

Tuesday morning Jack was on the docks doing his check of the boater's lines when his cell phone rang. It was Mary Robbins mother Barbara Collins calling from Pennsylvania.

She had heard from one of Mary's friends that Jack was asking questions about her disappearance. She said she had swallowed her pride and had called Gary, who had given her Jack's phone number.

Robbins had told her that Jack was going to solve the case and he would be exonerated. Barbara wanted to know what Jack had found out.

Sticking to the story he had consistently used with others who had questioned his motivation regarding the old case, Jack told her that he was looking into Mary's unsolved disappearance because it had been one of the first cases he had been involved with as a detective.

It was too early to say that he had any new facts regarding her disappearance that would solve it. Jack was sorry if the news had gotten her hopes up. He was not certain that there would be any new revelations regarding her daughter's disappearance.

While he had her on the phone, Jack asked Barbara if Mary had ever mentioned a friend named Vicky to her.

Barbara said that she could recall no Vicky, but in a letter she had written, Mary had mentioned a woman named Valerie. Mary had met her through a battered women's network that she had gotten involved with after Gary had become physical with her.

Mary did not disclose any details about her in the letter. She had only said that she had befriended a woman named Valerie. She found that it was very helpful emotionally to be able to share her fears with someone who had experienced similar occurrences.

Jack thanked her and took her phone number. He promised to call if he found anything.

Vicky was Valerie. Now he had a lead on Valerie's identity. He would contact the local Women's shelters and see if he could find out more about her through them.

He left to pick up the photos at the Jacob Dowe home located in Burlington's hill section. Gretchen Miller invited him in for a cup of coffee.

They started to talk about the day of Mary Robbins disappearance. Gretchen recalled again the two events that had remained in her memory.

First she had almost been run over by a boat while she was windsurfing, and then having to tell her father that her mother's car had been towed.

She related that Christy having remembered seeing Mary had reinforced her own memory of sighting of her on the path walking toward the marina.

She had pointed to the marina bathroom building for Christy and had seen Mary walking out of the development on the path to the point then.

Jack thanked her again for her help and left with the photos. It was still too early to stop and see Christy Sullivan so he decided to go down to Breakers for a club sandwich and beer to kill some time.

George Andrews was there meeting with his soon to be ex-son-in-law. He and Bob Brendon were sitting at a table located on the far edge of the outdoor dining area nearest the ferry docks. They were leaning toward each other talking in low voices so no one would overhear.

While Jack was waiting for his sandwich Bob stood up and said very loudly that he would not hesitate to open Pandora's Box and let out Georges secrets if George did not go along with his offer. He threw some money on the table and left. George's face was bright red. He was obviously very upset.

Jack hoped that he would not have a stroke as he certainly looked like he might. Andrews was still sitting at his table staring out at the breakwater when Jack finished his lunch and left the restaurant.

He left his truck parked on the waterfront and walked up Main Street hill the four blocks to Sully's. It was time to talk to Christy Sullivan and see if she could add anything to what he had already learned.

Christy was supervising the resetting of the dining room for the evening crowd when Jack arrived. They went into the lounge area and sat at a table.

Jack started the conversation. "Christy, thanks for taking the time to talk to me. I understand that you remember seeing Mary Robbins walking on the path to the point on the day that the pictures were taken."

"I've been thinking about that day a lot since the weekend." Christy said "I'm certain that it was Mary Robbins that I saw. I distinctly recall that she was walking quite quickly, almost jogging. She stopped on the path and looked behind her almost as if she was checking to see if anyone was following her."

"I waved to her she had already turned back around, so she didn't see me and didn't wave back. I continued to the bathroom."

"When I returned to the beach I looked up the path again. Mary could no longer be seen on the path. I figured that she was out for a jog, so she had gotten out of sight while I was in the bathroom."

Jack asked "Did you see anyone else on the path?"

"Not that I remember. I do recall seeing a Buick Gran Sport convertible drive into the marina. When I was in high school I had a crush on Louis O'Brien and thought it might be him."

"He and Conrad drove twin Buick Gran Sports in high school. I couldn't make out which of them it was, as they were driving pretty fast and I was already back on the beach below the road level when it went by."

"But I know that it went to the marina because I watched to see if it had been turning around. I went back up to the side of the road to in case it did."

"Did you see Mary come back down the path while you were watching for the car?"

"No, I never saw her again."

"Louis never seemed to notice me at school. I thought that if it was him and he saw how I looked in my bikini that it might make an impression on him. I had a really good body in high school and I hoped it would turn his head. The car didn't come back out of the marina however. I figured that he must be taking out his boat."

"After waiting several minutes I gave up and returned to my beach towel to tan until the police and tow trucks started to arrive."

"There had been some crazy lady running around telling everyone on the beach that they were going to be arrested for trespassing."

Jack thanked her and walked back down the hill to his truck. He would have to ask Conrad and Louis if either of them remembered going to the marina that day.

Perhaps one of them had seen Mary Robbins on the path returning from her walk. That could help confirm that she had disappeared during the night as had always been assumed and not earlier in the day. It was a long shot at best.

CHAPTER 34

When Jack got back to the marina, he found Eddie Michaels in front of the office involved in a heated discussion with Captain Crunch.

Paquette had shown up to take his boat out for a cruise on the lake and found it on his cradle instead of in its slip.

Jack told Eddie he could return to the gas dock. He started to explain to Paquette, "Sir, because of the incident that occurred the other night, you are no longer a boater/guest of the Marble Island Marina."

"What occurred on board your boat and on the docks was a blatant and unforgivable violation of the boater lease agreement, which states that no boater's behavior that interferes with another person's safety will be tolerated".

"Furthermore, no individual boaters' activities will be tolerated that interferes with other boaters right to peaceful enjoyment of the shared dock and marina facilities."

"The consequences of such actions or behaviors will result in immediate expulsion from the marina and forfeiture of any fees paid."

Paquette started to rant, "I've got important connections with a powerful judge. If you don't apologize to me and re-launch my boat immediately, I'll sue this two bit operation and end up owning Marble Island."

Jack told him "You can knock yourself out sir. The terms of usage are stated very clearly in the lease agreement that you signed. There were plenty of witnesses to your actions, not to mention the pending charges against you, as well as the police report."

Paquette finally left when Jack told him, "If you don't leave quietly right now, I'll call the Colchester Police ask them to add the charge of trespassing to your current problems."

"I'll see you in court Johnson," Paquette shouted and started to leave.

Jack replied calmly, "Sir, please note that according to the lease agreement you only have five more days of grace period before storage fees start to accrue on your boat. It would definitely behoove you to make arrangements to have it removed as soon as possible."

After he watched Paquette peel out of the parking lot in his silver GMC Sierra, Jack went into the office and called the other marina operators in the bay to give them the heads up on what had happened.

Most had already heard about the incident through the grape vine. Nick Griffith apologized to Jack again for not having warned him about Paquette.

He said that although he had known what a poor captain Paquette was he had not realized how unstable his personality was. Jack told Nick not to worry about it. As Newell Johnson had often stated … Everyone's hindsight always has 20-20 vision…

Jack checked with Eddie to make sure he was all right after his confrontation with Paquette. After confirming that other than being a little shaken up he was ok, he told Eddie to take the rest of the day off with pay. Jack would cover the remainder of his shift on the gas dock.

Things were usually slow on the bay on Tuesday afternoons. He had a few anglers stop for gas, and one Canadian sailboat that pulled in and rented a guest slip for a few days.

Jack pumped their holding tank, topped off their fuel and then directed them to an empty transient slip on the outer docks. He walked over and caught their lines, helping to tie them off for their stay.

When the young couple disembarked Jack showed them the cooking area and bath/laundry building. He handed them a key to the bath and laundry facilities and urged them to enjoy their stay in Malletts Bay.

It made Jack think about his dad who had been the consummate innkeeper, and the similarities between seeing to the wants and needs of transient boaters and those of traveling hotel guests.

The soul of Marble Island had not been destroyed in the fire that had razed the hotel. It remained in the waters of the lake on its docks. Newell Johnson was probably smiling down from heaven while watching his son act as host; he thought… The apple doesn't fall far from the tree…after all.

CHAPTER 35

Wednesday morning Jack woke up feeling very alone. He went to the Bayside Bakery and ordered a coffee and Danish pastry after taking a seat at the end of the counter.

He was not looking for conversation or company, just to be around other people. Occasionally, living alone led Jack to some feelings of mild depression. His psychiatrist had referred to this as Jack cocooning.

He had suggested that being near other people and watching their interactions would help Jack to deal with the occasional bouts of anxiety he felt from living with little social contact. It had helped in the past and he could tell already that it was working again today.

Jack had never been one to maintain a close friendship with anyone outside of his family. His social network had always been his siblings.

After his fathers' death he and Sally had hosted almost all of the holiday and birthday gatherings at their home. During these years of marriage, his younger brothers had become as close as or closer to Sally than to him.

As a result, after the divorce they had continued to include Sally in most family gatherings. Jack had told all of his brothers, and sister that he understood that the end of his marriage would not end their friendship with his ex-wife.

The only request that he had made was that when they invited Sally to a gathering that they not invite him, as he would not attend.

It had to do with the fact that she had never explained to him why she had wanted to end the marriage. Her only explanation was that they no longer brought out the best in each other.

During their 1 ½ year separation leading to their eventual divorce she had repeatedly refused to attend any counseling either as a couple or individually.

She had stated that she did not need any counseling, if there was a problem it was with Jack and he could go by himself.

When his youngest brother Matthew got married a few months after Jack's divorce, his fiancé had invited Sally to the wedding.

Jack had found out about the invitation and declined to attend because of it. It had made for hard feelings within the family.

Jack no longer had much contact with them with the exception of his older sister Carol and brother Tom. The incident had sent him back to therapy for several sessions.

The long-term effect of his divorce was that his formerly close relationship with his younger brothers had diminished to the point that they saw each other no more than a few times a year.

Jack found it hurtful to himself and so he had increasingly withdrawn from further interaction with them.

Doing this bit of self-psychoanalysis, Jack determined that the upcoming July 4th celebration was the reason for his current morose. He had told his mother that he would try to get everyone together on his boat for the fireworks.

The last time he had extended an invitation to the fireworks was two years ago. His brother Mark had told him that he had received a better offer and would not be attending. It still hurt like hell when Jack thought about it.

He wasn't looking forward to talking to Mark about this year. July 4th was a little over two weeks away. He needed to extend the invitations soon. He left the bakery to return to the marina. He had allowed himself enough self-pity for a while. It was time to get back to the realities of life.

Jack completed his daily routine on the docks before he called the Photo Garden to see if his photo enhancements had been returned from the out of state lab that they had been sent to.

He spoke to the owner, John Whalen, who told him that they would arrive at about three o'clock on the Fed Ex truck.

While he was waiting for the delivery, Jack decided to start contacting the women's shelters to see if he could find anything regarding the mysterious Valerie that Barbara Collins had identified as a friend of Mary Robbins.

Looking in the yellow pages under social services, Jack found several listings for groups that helped battered women. He started at the top and worked his way down.

After several strike outs, Jack was able to talk to a counselor at Women Helping Battered Women who had been working there in 1978 and remembered both Mary Robbins and Valerie.

She declined to answer any questions over the telephone, so he made an appointment to talk with her at 10:30 the next morning at her office on College Street in Burlington. There was no sense speculating about what he would find out.

Jack's dad had always admonished him with …don't put off until tomorrow that which you can accomplish today…

With that in mind, he called the Burlington Mayors office to make an appointment with Louis O'Brien for late afternoon. Then he called Conrad and asked him to meet him in the marina office.

When Conrad showed up at the office a few minutes later Jack told him his now well rehearsed retired detective cover story and asked him,

"Conrad, do you have any recollection of being at the Shelburne Marina on the day of Mary Robbins disappearance?"

"Where did that question come from? I can't recall, but it was a long time ago so that doesn't really surprise me. Your question certainly does though."

"I often went to the marina when I was in high school. The Donzi was kept in a slip there. My cousin Louis and I had shared using it to water ski and cruise around on the lake."

"I have no idea whether or not I was using it on the day that Mary Robbins disappeared but it is certainly possible that I was. I think I might have had her as an English teacher, but I'm not sure."

"Conrad, it was just a long shot. I didn't really expect you to remember all the details of a day from 27 years ago."

"Not to change the subject Jack, but I've changed my mind about giving the Donzi to my fiancé. I've decided to sell it instead. A buddy told me that Miami Florida is the best market for it. I'll be arranging to have it shipped down in a few weeks. In the meantime you should drain the fuel and prepare it for shipping overland."

"What about Tony Kravitz' interest in buying the boat? Tony would probably be willing to match any other offer, and you wouldn't have the additional expense of shipping the boat to Florida."

"We've already discussed that Jack. I told you that I would burn the boat before letting Tony Kravitz own it."

His tone of voice immediately made Jack decide to keep his knowledge of Louis's interest in the Donzi from Conrad.

Jack would tell Louis about Conrad's change in plans for the boat. He would let the cousin's deal with it among themselves.

It was time for Jack to head downtown to pick up his photo enhancement and then to go meet the mayor.

CHAPTER 36

Jack drove downtown and parked his truck in the city parking garage on the corner of Cherry Street and South Winooski Avenue. He walked the two blocks to the Photo Garden, went inside, and picked up the envelope with the enhanced photo.

Without even taking the time to open the manila envelope containing the photo enhancement Jack thanked John Whalen for his assistance with it and left the shop. He would study it later.

City Hall was just around the corner and down the block at the corner of Church Street and Main Street. Jack walked in and took the stairs to the second floor where the mayor's office was.

Elaine Hannigan was the mayor's secretary. It was a post she had held for over thirty years. She had served first a Democratic mayor, next a Republican, then a Progressive, and now another Democratic …His Honor Louis O'Brien IV…

Jack had met her years ago while on the police force. He said hello and took a seat against the wall in her small office. After a few minutes, Louis walked out of his office and greeted Jack.

The mayor asked if the visit was official city business, when Jack replied that it was not, Louis took a cell phone off from the corner of Elaine's desk and told her that he and Jack were going for a short walk around City Hall Park. He should be back in about 30 minutes.

She assured him that she would call if anything came up. Louis and Jack walked down the stairs and exited through the back doors, which abutted the park.

Louis asked "What is it that brings you to Burlington to see me?"

Jack responded, "Louis, the first case I had as a detective is still unsolved. It was the Mary Robbins disappearance. I have been bothered by it for years and recently started looking into it again. Your name and Conrad's have come up. I'd like to ask you a few questions about what you might know regarding it. Any knowledge that you have might be helpful."

"Christy Sullivan remembers seeing a Buick Gran Sport convertible going to Shelburne Shipyard on the day of Mary Robbins disappearance. She wasn't certain whether it was you or Conrad driving as your cars were identical.

Louis asked, "How did Christy recognize the car and how is she certain that it was either Conrad or myself?"

She had a big crush on you and watched for the car to come back through. She was hoping that you'd see her in her bathing suit and fall in lust with her."

Louis's laughter broke the tension that had been building between them.

"By my senior year in high school I was hopelessly in love with Martha and didn't give a second look to anyone else. I will have to stop by Sully's and see if Christy will give me a campaign donation sometime soon."

"Just be sure to take Martha with you and buy her an expensive dinner. That way everything will appear on the up and up, Martha will know that there's nothing going on between you and Christy, and Christy will know that you're happily married."

They went back to the question about being at the marina on the day that Mary had disappeared. Louis said, "It couldn't have been me Jack."

"I took all of my final exams early my senior year and was attending a Buick Dealer Council Meeting in Orlando Florida with my dad. Uncle Frank had arranged it all so that I could chaperone my father. It was an exciting trip."

"I got to ride around the Petty training track, which was located next to Disney World. Dale Earnhart Sr. was driving a Buick Regal in the NASCAR series and had attended the dealer meeting as guest speaker."

"Earnhart brought his short track car with him and offered fast laps to anyone who was interested. I took three turns."

"I even got an autographed picture of him standing next to me. It's still hanging in the customer waiting lounge at the dealership."

Jack thanked Louis for his time. As he started walking away, he remembered the Donzi. "Louis, Conrad told me this morning that he's going to ship the Donzi to Miami and sell it. You asked me to let you know when he grew tired of it. I guess it didn't take him long."

"Do me a favor, when you talk to him about it please don't bring up my name."

Louis promised him that his name would not be mentioned and thanked him for the heads up.

Jack walked up Church Street. He stopped at Ben and Jerry's for a vanilla ice cream cone on his way back to the parking garage.

He paid his parking fee and drove his truck home to the marina. After dinner, he would enjoy a cigar and study the photo to see what it would tell him.

Dinner was potato salad that Jack picked up at Mazza's deli counter and a diet ice tea. He wanted to be able to devote his full attention to the photo so he turned off his cell phone.

He climbed the ships ladder to the upper deck on his boat with a cold Excel and a Fuente cigar. He settled in and opened the package from the photo lab.

What he saw was a bit of a surprise and a bit of a letdown. There was a young couple in a white and yellow Donzi speeding by heading north on the lake. Jack recognized the boat immediately.

He had just restored it for Conrad. What he could not tell for certain was which of the cousin's was in the boat.

He knew that it must be Conrad, because of his conversations with him and Louis earlier in the day. He wished that the face of his passenger were recognizable. If Conrad could see the young woman's features, he might be able to recall her name.

Jack would have someone else to ask if they had seen Mary Robbins that day. All he could do was show the picture to Conrad and see if it might jog his memory.

As his father had said on many occasions …Two steps forward, one step back… Perhaps tomorrow with the counselor at the women's shelter would bear some fruit.

CHAPTER 37

Thursday morning Jack went through his marina duties quickly so he would be on time for his 10:30 appointment at the women's shelter. He arrived a few minutes early.

He was the only male in the waiting room. He found it a rather hostile environment. At 10:30 sharp, a woman came out of the back and called Jack's name.

Jack stood up and as he approached the woman, he extended his hand to shake hers. She looked at him coldly and introduced herself.

Her name was Pamela Abbott. Jack ignored the slight and followed her down the hall to her office. He could not help but wonder what her story was. She obviously had very little use for men Jack thought; someone must have hurt her badly.

No matter. He was here to get all the information he could about Mary Robbins and hopefully Valerie as well. If he could convince Pamela that he was a "good guy," she might be able to provide it.

It was time to be honest about his interest. A bad cover story would not be convincing to an experienced counselor. She would know if he was being sincere or trying to shine her on.

He started at the beginning. He spoke nonstop for about fifteen minutes finished by asking "Could you help me find Valerie so I can see if she knows anything about Mary's disappearance?"

Pamela had a file folder lying on her desk. She opened it up and studied its contents for several minutes before looking up. Finally, she said:

"I'll try to help. But I cannot and will not violate anyone's privacy. What I can agree to do is to attempt to locate Valerie and explain your interest in speaking with her. There are no guarantees that she will agree to talk with you".

"It's been 27 years since our last and only contact. Valerie moved out of state and changed her identity. She left secretly in the middle of the night."

"Even I was not aware of her plan in advance. I received a letter from her a few weeks after she left. Valerie left on the same night as Mary Robbins disappearance."

"I had overheard the pair talking about disappearing together previously after a group session. I had not taken their conversation seriously. It had not sounded like an impending plan. It was more like a daydream."

"Valerie's boyfriend had beaten the hell out of her several times. He had also physiologically abused her over a long period. Valerie's history had paralleled Mary's."

"They had been close in group therapy sessions. When Mary disappeared at the same time Valerie did, it had seemed likely that they might have gone away together."

"The story of Mary Robbins disappearance was widely reported in the newspaper as well as on the local TV news broadcasts. The investigation was focused on Gary Robbins. After a few weeks with no reported progress in the case I was about to come forward."

"That's when I received the letter from Valerie saying that she was safe after leaving Burlington secretly. I decided that if Gary Robbins was guilty of harming Mary it would be proven by the investigation going on."

"To reveal that Valerie had disappeared at the same time and had been a friend of Mary's could cast a lot of doubt on Gary's guilt. He was a wife abuser and deserved the trouble he was in for that fact alone."

"If Mary had in fact run away like Valerie had, it would do no harm to anyone for me to remain mum. It could hurt Mary and Valerie if I came forward. So I never spoke of it to anyone else. To do otherwise would have been a betrayal of their trust, and likely would have placed them both in danger again. Over the years, I had thought less and less about it. That was until you called yesterday and asked about Mary and Valerie."

Jack gave Pamela his cell phone number. He asked her "Please try to forward this to Valerie. When you communicate with her you should tell Valerie that she need not contact me if she knows that Mary is safe somewhere."

"Just have her contact Mary and ask her to contact her parents and let them know. They would never tell Gary Robbins or anyone else who might harm her."

"If, however Mary did not leave with her, I hope that Valerie will contact me. She can block her phone number. I don't need to know where she is; just that Mary did not go with her."

"As Valerie's name had never come up in the investigation, or in the years since, she need not be involved now unless she has knowledge about what had happened to Mary."

Pamela assured Jack that she would try her best. After that, whatever happened would be up to Valerie.

She would call him if she were successful in contacting Valerie. No news would mean she had been unable to make contact. Pamela was going to shred the file today.

Jack thanked her and left. He understood that her commitment to her clients took precedence over anything else. She would protect them at all costs, including interfering with a police investigation.

It would do absolutely no good to threaten her, especially all these years later. He admired her dedication to her profession and to the women she was helping. It reminded him of his own sense of purpose when he had been on the force.

All he could do now was to play the waiting game. He was certainly becoming used to it. That was the story of his life since he had started on this ride.

CHAPTER 38

Friday started another busy weekend at Marble Island Marina. In addition to the regular boaters, Jack and the crew had to prepare for an "open house" event for the public.

The Realtor that Conrad had contracted with to market the home sites and condominiums on the island wanted to display the marina facilities that would be available to them as part of their home purchase.

This translated to a lot of extra work for the marina staff. They had to spit shine everything that was in public view.

It also meant that Conrad would be hanging around all weekend to play gracious owner/operator. As he knew virtually nothing of the actual operation, Jack would have to remain close enough to bail him out when someone asked a question that he could not answer. That would be almost any question asked.

The positive aspect of the ordeal for Jack was that he loved talking to people who were interested in boating, Lake

Champlain and its history, the environment, fishing, or almost any other related topic.

At least it would keep him from thinking too much about a phone call that might not come. Newell Johnson would have referred to it as … The silver lining in the cloud…

During a lull in the action on Saturday afternoon, Jack reopened the conversation he had with Conrad about Mary Robbins disappearance. He showed him the picture he had had blown up of the Donzi and asked

"Conrad, do you recognize the young woman that was riding in the boat with you?"

Conrad stared mutely at the photo for several minutes before replying.

"That is not me in the boat. It must have been Louis. I would certainly remember it if I had been using the boat that day and who I was with."

"Conrad, Louis was in Florida with his father during exam week, it must have been you in the boat."

" No it wasn't, I repeat, I would remember if it was me, one of the Shelburne Shipyard employees must have taken the boat out for a joy ride. I had exams that week and would have been either at school taking one, or studying at home. I was struggling with my grades and my father had come down hard on me."

"My father had wanted me to be accepted at an Ivy League College. The only school that had accepted me for the fall semester was Paul Smith University in rural New York State."

"Dad and I had gone to Princeton where he had graduated years earlier. The purpose of our trip was to convince the admissions office to make an exception for me if I could show immediate improvement. "

'Princeton had agreed that if I could do well in my final exams, and would attend some summer courses that they would accept me on probationary status in the fall. I worked my ass off for that chance."

Jack knew that this special consideration had cost Charles a four year scholarship commitment for a needy student. He had apparently made it abundantly clear to Conrad that if he failed to get into Princeton he could forget that he was a member of the O'Brien family.

Jack also knew that Conrad had barely graduated from Princeton. Newell Johnson had spoken about it to him one time when the two of them were discussing the low likelihood of business's being successfully handed down from one generation to the next.

The O'Brien's had always defied the odds in the past, if you excluded Louis III, but Newell did not think that Conrad had the makings of an innkeeper. Consequently, he felt that the future of the Marble Island Resort was in jeopardy when Charles was gone.

Jack had often felt grateful that Newell had not lived to see his prediction come to pass after Charles death and the fire that had destroyed the hotel.

Conrad's story seemed believable, but did not jive with what he had said just a week before, when he had said that he could not remember anything from that far back.

Something about the picture had disturbed Conrad. Perhaps he did recognize the girl and was embarrassed as to her identity so Conrad was denying any knowledge of ever being with her.

Jack was certain of one thing. It had to be either Conrad or Louis in the boat. They looked a lot alike. There was enough detail in the photo to know that it had been one or the other at the helm. The O'Brien family resemblance was unmistakable.

Conrad announced that he was coming down with a migraine headache and left the marina to go home to bed. Jack knew he was upset about their conversation.

It was very unlike Conrad to use an excuse to duck out of his duties as real estate mogul. That was an unexpected turn of events.

The rest of the weekend went quickly. Jack was able to re-lease Paquette's vacated slip to his personal physician, Rick Tomassi. They had a great doctor patient relationship. Jack had not seen a personal physician for many years prior to his heart attack.

He had assumed that the annual physical paid for by the police department would find any health problems that existed. Things had changed with the disease. He started to see Rick regularly and they had developed a close relationship. Rick was as close to a good friend as Jack had.

Rick had recently divorced. He ex-wife had taken him to the cleaners, getting possession of most of their marital assets, including their home on the lake in Shelburne.

The divorce had taken two years to complete and had cost him plenty. After the first year in limbo, Rick had bought a small condominium in South Burlington to move into.

Now remarried, he and his new wife Paula were in the market for a single family home. They had come to Marble Island thinking that a custom build would best suit their desires. Lake access was a bonus.

Rick had a twenty foot ski boat. It was a little small to really need a slip, but having it in the water when he wanted to go out would be much easier than having to launch it from its trailer.

Jack welcomed them to the marina, showed them around, gave them their key to the bath/laundry facilities, and started to joke with Paula that a great belated wedding present for Rick would be a nice 34 foot Pearson sail boat, and he happened to have one on consignment from the owner sitting in the storage yard. Paula said she would wait until next season and see if he was worth it.

Jack then turned serious and told her that Rick's care was the reason he was still alive, and how much he appreciated it. He congratulated them on their marriage, thanked them for joining the Marble Island family, and walked them to their car.

Newell had taught his children to always be polite and to be appreciative of help from others. Jack tried to practice that lesson whenever possible.

They were the last remaining open house visitors, so Jack took down the signs, and sent his crew home. He finished shutting down the gas dock, locked the office door, and went down the dock to his houseboat to have dinner and relax with a DVD.

The DVD was season two of CSI Miami, one of Jacks favorite TV shows. He was amused with the way that Horiatio Caine and his team always found the incriminating evidence to arrest the criminals.

If only the criminal justice system was truly that efficient. Wouldn't it be great if Jack could identify some DNA evidence that would solve Mary Robbins disappearance, or Bennie Richards' death?

Somewhere in the middle of one of the episodes on the disc, one of the CSI's had stated something that stuck in Jack's mind… Everything old is new again… That really summed up his feelings about his current activities. He fell asleep on his couch with the TV playing. Maybe he could figure things out in his dreams.

CHAPTER 39

Monday morning, just another day in paradise, Jack thought as he went through his routine. Maybe today his phone would ring and he could connect a few more dots in his current puzzle.

While he was waiting, he could find plenty to do.

He started by taking the gasoline transfer tank to the shed to drain the tank on the Donzi. He pumped out about 32 of the 40 gallons that he had put in to fill the boat the previous week. It figured to about 6 mpg Jack calculated. That was pretty respectable for a muscle boat.

He pulled the transfer tank over to the gasoline storage tank and pumped out its contents. Then he put the transfer tank back on the gas dock next to the fuel hut.

Next, he loaded the old carpeting and upholstery in a garden way cart that the marina supplied for boaters to transport their gear and supplies from the parking lot to their boats on the docks.

He pushed the cart over to the dumpster and tossed the contents away. On his way back to the shed to get the old flooring materials, his cell phone rang.

Pamela Abbott was on the other end of the cell signal. She had talked to Valerie over the weekend. Jack could expect a call around noontime. Valerie had not even known that Mary Robbins had disappeared.

Jack put away the cart in the parking lot with the others and went to the office. One of his possible scenarios had just blown up. He wondered if Valerie had information that could help him confirm one of the remaining ones.

He started writing down all the questions that he wanted to ask her when she called. He thought he would only have one chance to talk with her and he needed to cover as much as he could.

He would start with when the last time was that Valerie had spoken to Mary. Had Mary ever give Valerie any indication that she actually feared for her safety while living with Gary?

Had Mary talked about leaving Gary? If so, did she say where she would go?

Did Valerie know if Mary had been having an affair?

If she did know of an affair, did she know with whom? Did Valerie think that Mary might have taken off with her lover? Did she know of any reason that Mary would not have contacted even her parents if she were alive?

Could Valerie think of anyone else that Mary might have confided in?

Lastly, had Mary known that Valerie was going to disappear that day?

The answers to those questions would hopefully help Jack determine what had really happened to Mary Robbins.

The answer to that mystery would hopefully lead to the break he was looking for in the death of Bennie Richards.

Just another day in paradise he thought again. But, was it paradise lost?

At 11 A.M., Conrad made an appearance at the marina office. He wanted to talk some more about the day Mary Robbins had gone missing.

He had thought about it while resting at home on Sunday. He admitted that quite possibly he had been out on the boat that day, but for the life of him he could not recall for sure.

He had not meant to be so defensive when Jack had shown him the picture. During his senior year in high school, he had been sneaking around with a 15 year old girl who had been working at the hotel as a chambermaid.

It must have been her on the boat with him. It was so embarrassing to him even now that Conrad had overreacted to Jack's questions when he had shown him the picture.

Conrad did not want anyone to know about the incident, even after all of these years. His father Charles had bought off the girl's parents and kept everything quiet. He hoped Jack would understand.

Jack told Conrad that Newell Johnson had told him about the underage girl situation at the time that it had occurred.

The conversation between Jack and his father had been in confidence, so Jack had never spoken about it with anyone else.

He felt certain that no one else need know that the incident had happened. It was old news. If Conrad could let him know the girl's name, he would contact her confidentially.

All he wanted to ask her about was if she had seen Mary Robbins that day, and if so, where she had appeared to be headed.

Conrad said that after all the years that had passed by, he could not even remember the girl's name. He might be able to find it in Charles's papers.

Her parents had threatened a statutory rape charge and had ended up signing a confidentiality agreement in exchange for a $10,000 payment. The agreement might still be around somewhere with some of his father's personal papers.

On the other hand, it might have been destroyed in the fire when the old hotel burned down. All of the employee payroll and personnel records had been burned in the blaze.

Conrad was not sure what else was stored in the hotel storage room with them. He told Jack he would start searching in the attic of the house where he had stored Charles' personal things after he had died. Jack thanked Conrad for his honesty and his help.

As Conrad left the marina office Jack's cell phone started to ring. He looked at the caller ID. He saw Restricted on the screen where the phone number displayed. He answered and the women on the other end introduced herself as Valerie.

After introducing himself and thanking her for calling, Jack started with the list of questions he had prepared. Valerie said that she had spoken to Mary at mid-morning on the day that she had escaped from Burlington.

Originally, Valerie had not planned to leave for another few weeks, but her boyfriend had tried to break into her apartment the previous evening while she had been at Mary's for dinner. That had caused her to move her plans up.

She had called Mary to let her know so Mary would not come over to spend the night and find her not at home. She had not confided in anyone else about her plan for leaving.

She said that Mary was not really afraid for her safety living with Gary. After the first time that he had beat her up, he had just ignored her when they were at home together.

Mary had planned to file for divorce after she had hidden away enough money to sustain her for several months. She had told Valerie that she knew that it would be an ugly divorce and Gary would try to make sure Mary ended up with nothing.

She wanted to stay in Burlington and fight for what she deserved for putting up with him. She was not planning to move away.

Valerie was certain that Mary had been having an affair, but she had never admitted to it. There was a change in her demeanor a few months before Valerie had left. It was a softening in her attitude about men.

Valerie had tried to talk Mary into going with her when she left but Mary would not consider it because of the ties she felt to Burlington.

There was no one else other than Pamela Abbott that she could think of that Mary would have confided in. Her parents had never been supportive of the marriage.

Mary's mother took every opportunity to tell her what a mistake she had made after Mary had told her about Gary's beating her up. She did not feel that she could go back to Pennsylvania to stay with them because of their "holier than thou" attitudes.

The last thing Mary had said to Valerie was to wish her luck and to urge her not to try to contact her directly. Mary said she would tell Pamela about Valerie's decision to leave Burlington, and Valerie should let Pamela know that she was all right after she was settled, as it would be safer for her to communicate with her than with Mary.

Jack thanked Valerie for trusting enough to call him. She replied that she was very sorry that she had not learned of Mary's disappearance until now.

Except for the note she had sent Pamela, she had cut off all contact with Burlington. It had been a very painful part of her life and she had not wanted to ever think of it again. With that, the conversation ended.

CHAPTER 40

Jack put his cell phone back into his pocket and walked outside. He needed to digest what Valerie had told him and decide how to continue.

While her information had not pointed directly to Gary and seemed to lessen the possibility of a violent end in his marriage to Mary, it had not eliminated him as a suspect either. It was time to look for Mary's phantom lover.

Jack was going to need a few reference materials to find some more leads. He told Eddie Michaels that he would be off site for a few hours, and walked to his truck. A drive to Burlington High School was first on his agenda.

He parked in the visitor area of the parking lot and walked inside to the administrative office. He asked the secretary if he could purchase a yearbook from 1978.

She explained that the school was not involved with the sale of yearbooks. That had always been a student activity. Jack could however find a copy of all of the old yearbooks in the school library.

After thanking her for her help and getting directions to the library, Jack went back out to his truck for a legal pad that he kept in the cab. He re-entered the school and walked through the corridors to the library. There were many kids in the hallways because summer school had started the previous week.

Jack entered the library and asked the librarian on duty where he would find the old yearbooks. She directed him to a shelving unit over on the back wall.

He pulled out the 1978 yearbook and the current one as well. He was looking for teachers from 1978 that were still working there so he could ask them what they remembered about Mary Robbins.

He was hoping that her lover had been involved with the school and someone would have noticed something that would allow Jack to identify him. Slowly going back and forth between the yearbooks, Jack made a list of three teachers still working there who had been colleagues of Mary's.

He also went through the 1978 yearbook thoroughly to read any comments that referred to Mary made by the students or faculty at the time. He knew that often the student body was more aware of a teacher/teacher romance than their fellow teachers were.

When Jack had been a high school student there had been a romantic tryst going on between a history teacher and an assistant principal.

The rest of the faculty had been oblivious, but some of the kids in the student body had been very aware of what was going on. The couple was busted together one weekend at the assistant principal's house. The police showed up with a search warrant to investigate a neighbor's tip.

The assistant principal had been growing marijuana on his upstairs porch and his plants had been spotted by one of his neighbors. Both he and the history teacher had lost their teaching certifications.

In today's world they would not even lose their jobs, but 35 years previously even marijuana possession was a felony charge and meant a criminal record that would remain with them for the rest of their lives, making it impossible for either to teach again.

He was now a carpenter in St. Albans. She had moved back to Newport and worked in her father's hardware store.

Jack found a few student comments about Mary Robbins. One in particular caught his interest. A senior named Michael Meyers wanted to nominate her for a special award that he proposed for ... sexiest teacher you'd like to see in a wet tee shirt... Probably just a horny kid with a crush on a teacher but worth looking into, Jack decided.

He also wrote down the names of the co-editors of the yearbook. It could be worthwhile to talk with them to see what they could recall. They would have had their hands on the pulse of the graduating class and faculty.

When Jack got back into his truck, he placed a call to Robbins Auto Parts on North Winooski Avenue and asked to speak to Gary. He was only on hold for a minute before Robbins picked up.

Jack asked him if he could get the list of students that Mary had been tutoring. Gary had mentioned that he had kept it with her other school things since her disappearance. Robbins said he would look for it when he got home that evening.

Jack asked if he could stop by his house and pick it up after dinnertime. They agreed they would meet at 7:30 P.M. at his house. He still lived in the development on Shelburne Point.

Jack went back to his boat. The last time he had taken it out it had started to misfire a bit on the way back to the docks. He had picked up a new distributor cap, rotor, wires and a set of spark plugs the next day and stored them on the boat.

Turning off his thoughts about the Robbins case, while tuning up the motor on his boat, would help to kill the time until evening. He finished up working on his engine in 1 ½ hours.

He cast off from the dock and took a short cruise out to the railroad fill and back. The old scow was purring like a happy kitten on catnip.

Jack took a shower and dressed in his best jeans and a polo shirt. He thought he might stop by Breakers on his way back from Shelburne for a sandwich and beer.

He might even run into someone he knew. The last time he was there, he had shared a cigar with the mayor.

He drove down to Shelburne Point and arrived a little before 7 P.M. Because he was so early, he went past the street that Robbins lived on and into the Shelburne Shipyard parking lot. He locked his truck up and walked back to the entrance at the road.

He took a right on the old pathway toward the nude beach on the end of the point. He slowly walked along next to the chain link fence that had recently been installed between the path and the new homes that had been built when the Webb family had sold the property a few years ago.

Leanne Wilson and her husband should have bought one of the lots on the point, Jack thought. They all had direct lake access.

There was no one on the beach when Jack reached the end of the path after ten minutes of walking slowly. He stopped for a minute and looked out at Juniper Island.

He recalled how 22 years before he had purchased his first and only big sailboat from CanAm Yachts. They had operated out of the shipyard. His Brother Tom's father-in-law, Mel Merrill, was the owner.

Jack and Sally had owned a sixteen-foot day sailor that they had purchased at the start of the 1983 boating season and he had discovered his love of the water.

When Mel had seen it at Tom's house one Sunday, he told Jack that he had a great boat for him that he could even play house on.

Jack had driven down to the shipyard that evening to look at the 25 footer and left knowing that he would be its next owner. It was small enough to single hand, and large enough to cruise the lake with.

Sally had not thought that they could afford it. The deal was closed three weeks later when Mel called and said that he would finance it for them.

It was a thousand dollars down and whatever they could afford per month after that. No interest and no set term on the time for repayment. They had finished paying it off eight months later with Sally's first real estate commission check.

The day they had picked it up at the shipyard to sail up to Tom's, where they were going to keep it on a mooring in front of his house, Jack had left the detachable swim ladder loose on deck next to the mast. He made his first tack a little south of Juniper Island and the jib sheet had caught on the ladder and pulled it overboard into the lake. It sank immediately into 340 feet of water.

Jack had continued sailing that boat until he had suffered his heart attack after his divorce. It was the only thing he had left the marriage with other than his truck, a few Johnson family heirlooms, and his clothes.

His cardiologist had strongly recommended that he give up sailing alone on the lake. Needing a place to live, he had sold the sailboat and bought his current home on the water.

Jack looked at his watch. It was 7:15 P.M. It was time to visit Gary Robbins and pick up the list. He quickened his pace on the way back to his truck. Jack pulled into the Robbins driveway at 7:28 P.M. and knocked on his front door.

When Gary answered the door, he had a drink in his hand and offered Jack one. Jack declined, telling him that he did not drink anymore.

They sat down in the living room and Gary leaned over and started to go through a box that was sitting beside the chair he was in.

After a minute of rummaging through the contents, he pulled out a small notebook and handed it to Jack. He opened it and saw that it was the first page of a ledger.

There was a student's name at the top of the first page. Below the name on the left side of the page was the date and time of each tutoring appointment. The right side of the page showed the amount Mary had charged for her lessons. Beside each amount was written the date that she had received payment.

A quick glance showed about twenty pages filled with the information. He would need a little time with the 1978 year book to match the names to students.

Gary told Jack that he was welcome to take the notebook with him. Jack asked if he could borrow the other contents of the box as well. Robbins had no objection so he placed the notebook back into the top of the box put on the cover and stood up.

He started to walk to the front door. He turned at the door and thanked Robbins for his help. He would return everything after a few days time when he had had an opportunity to study it all.

CHAPTER 41

Jack placed the box of Mary's papers and miscellaneous belongings behind the seat in his cab. He drove to the Burlington waterfront, parked, and locked his truck in Breakers parking lot.

A ferry came in as he walked down the quay to the bar/restaurant. It was a busy Monday night, so Jack ended up sitting on an empty stool at the outdoor bar.

Fortunately, it was at the end of the bar near the ferry slip so Jack would not be bothering people with the after dinner Fuente cigar he planned to enjoy while watching the sunset.

He ordered a cheeseburger with fries and cole slaw to eat, and an Excel to go with it. There was a small cover band combo playing oldies on the little stage to the right of the bar.

The music was enjoyable and several couples were dancing. What a great setting for a movie he thought. No wonder Burlington was constantly winning recognition as one of

America's most livable cities. Scenes like this were right out of a travel brochure.

His dinner arrived and Jack settled in to enjoy it. The combo was playing "My Girl" a late 60's hit. He ordered another beer and distributed the condiments on his burger.

A voice behind him said hello and he turned around. It was his high school sweetheart. Her name was Kelly Cosgrove. It had been a long time.

When Jack had found out that she was dating someone else after he had left for his service in the Navy he had written her a long letter, asking her wait for him.

He had wanted them to get married when he came home on leave after his basic training and had proposed to her before he had left.

Her father had been the one to push her into dating others, telling her that she and Jack were too young to get married. He had a tremendous amount of influence over her.

She was a year younger than Jack was. Still in her senior year of high school, she had met a college student named Bob Bennett, while at her part time job. He pursued her hard, even showing up at her parent's house to see her uninvited.

Although her father, Dave had not liked Bob much, he had encouraged Kelly to go out with him, figuring that it might divert her feelings toward Jack. It had worked beyond Dave's expectations. Kelly had fallen in love with Bob, and Jack was the recipient of a "Dear John" letter.

A year later, when he learned that Kelly and Bob were getting married, Jack had gone to the Cosgrove house to see her while home on a two week leave before shipping out overseas.

Jack had learned that Bob Bennett was nothing more than a spoiled kid who would always be looking for someone else to take care of him. He had tried to convince her that marrying him was a mistake. He failed.

Jack went back to the Navy licking his wounded pride, and put his love for Kelly away in the back of his mind.

Over the years, he had kept in touch with her family. Two of her sisters were hair stylists. When her father bankrolled a styling salon that the family ran, Jack always went there for his monthly haircuts. He saw her parents occasionally at church when he attended with his mother.

He had been married to Sally for five years when he heard about Kelly's divorce. He knew he had to keep his distance from her or his own marriage would be jeopardized. Each month he received an update on her life from one of her sisters during his haircut. She had a few relationships, but nothing that became permanent.

A few years before his divorce from Sally, Kelly's family had closed the hair salon and Jack had lost touch with them. He had no other excuse to check up on her well-being.

This was the first time they had spoken to each other in thirty-four years. He could not see that her appearance had changed at all. She invited him to join her at her table.

Her sister Heather was with her and had spotted Jack at the bar. Heather had pointed him out to Kelly and suggested that she go over and say hello.

She said that it had taken a few minutes for her to work up her nerve before she had come over. When she heard "My Girl", she knew that she should. It had been "their song" in high school.

Jack told her that he would love to sit down and catch up on things. He grabbed his food and drink, left a tip on the bar and followed her back to her table.

They talked for two hours before Heather, who had been mostly ignored during the conversation had insisted that Kelly take her home. She had to be at work at the bank where she was employed the next morning at 7:00 A.M. Jack walked them to their car.

As he held Kelly's door for her, he asked if he could call her sometime. She wrote down her phone number and told him that she looked forward to hearing from him. It was a great end to the day.

CHAPTER 42

Jack slept better on Monday night than he had in a long time. He woke up on Tuesday morning feeling optimistic.

The marina was in good shape so his morning routine went quickly. As soon as he'd finished, Jack took the notebook out of Mary Robbins' box which he had placed in his boat next to the one containing Bennie Richards' things when he'd gotten back to his boat the previous night. He had put the paper with Kelly Cosgrove's phone number on his refrigerator with a magnet.

He left a note in the marina office reminding Eddie that the Boat Works would be delivering Dr. Rick's ski boat and instructing him to put it in the former Captain Crunch slip.

It was past 9:00 A.M and he was anxious to get to work on the notebook at the Burlington High School Library. Matching up names with faces from the yearbook should be fairly easy work.

The sooner he finished with it, the sooner he would be able to locate the former tutees to see if they could help him uncover any additional information about Mary Robbins.

Work progressed nicely at the library. Jack started with the name of the student on the first page and looked through the senior pictures until he picked out the correct image.

He copied down the former student's information from the caption under the photo on his notepad and moved on to the next.

A few of the identities slowed him down, as they had been underclassmen. Because of that, there was no information about where they were going to college, or what their future plans were. It would mean following up in other yearbooks.

Michael Meyers had been one of the students she had tutored. Because of the comment he had made about how sexy Mary Robbins was, Jack decided to move his name to the top of his list.

Looking at his tutoring schedule with her, he saw that they had met once a week at 7:30 P.M. for a sixty-minute session. She had stopped tutoring him in January 1978.

An hour after starting Jack had only five or six pages left. He finished up the page with a sophomore named Karen Brown on it and turned to the next.

Conrad O'Brien. The name stared back at him from the top of the page. Jack studied the records and saw that Conrad had been working with Mary for tutoring help for two years.

Their schedule, according to the ledger, had been to meet twice each week for ninety minute sessions. Most of their appointments were scheduled for the 4:30 P.M. time slots.

In January 1978, there was an increase in the number of appointments to three each week. The time of the appointments had changed to 5:30 P.M.

The need to increase the appointments jived with what Conrad had told Jack about the extra effort that he had had to put out to raise his grades so he would be able to attend Princeton.

The fact that he had being seeing Mary Robbins for tutoring help for two years and had not informed Jack of this relationship was very disturbing.

Conrad was well aware that he was looking into Mary's disappearance. There was no reason for him to have withheld the information from Jack. He knew immediately that he needed to tread softly.

He would check into the other names, especially Michael Meyers, before confronting Conrad with this information.

Their current relationship was strained enough. Jack didn't want to find himself looking for a job and new marina to live at unless there was cause to rock the boat.

Another idiom from Newell Johnson came to mind. ….If you shake up a hornet's nest, you should expect to be stung…

Where had his early morning optimism disappeared to so quickly? He hoped it had not gone to hang out with Mary Robbins ghost.

He finished with the last four students in the notebook. Next, he went to the shelves and took out the appropriate ones to follow through with as much information as he could glean from them.

When he had finished with his work, he stopped at the librarian's desk and thanked her for all of her help on his way back to his truck. It was almost noontime.

He decided to go out on the lake for the afternoon and sort through the rest of the items in Mary Robbins' box without any distractions. He returned to the marina, checked in with Eddie to make sure things were under control, and boarded his houseboat.

He cast off his lines and headed out to the open lake. He had decided to travel north to Valcour Island. It had been the site of naval battles between America and England in both the Revolutionary War and the War of 1812. It was a well known historical fact that those battles had turned the tide against the British Empire in each of the wars.

CHAPTER 43

Jack steered his boat into the northern cove at Lighthouse Point on the western side of Valcour Island. He maneuvered in until he was close to shore as it only drew 3 ½ feet of water.

That would allow the cruising sailboats that frequented the anchorage for overnight stays to find suitable anchorages in deeper water further from shore when they started to show up in another hour or so.

He went below to the cabin after confirming that his anchor had set safely He fixed himself a peanut butter and jelly sandwich. He brought his sandwich and a diet ice tea out to the upper deck along with Mary Robbins' box of materials.

He stared at the box without taking any action to open it while he pushed his sandwich around his plate and drank his ice tea.

After 15 minutes of playing with his food, Jack lit up a cigar, consulted his notes, and started to call the teachers who had taught with Mary and were still working at BHS.

None of them knew or suspected that she had been having an affair. Mary had not socialized with her fellow teachers much. She was younger that most of them and the consensus was that she had more rapport with her students than with the faculty. After the last phone call was completed, Jack opened the box.

He reached inside and took out the papers, setting them down on the table, and started to read through them. Most at the top of the stack had to do with her teaching career. They were outlines for lesson plans, book lists of suggested reading, and other teaching aids.

About halfway through the stack, Jack started getting into correspondence that Mary had saved from her friends and family. 1978 had been several years before people had personal computers and email had started to become mainstream.

He found a few letters from her mother, the last of which expressed her feelings about Mary's marriage to Gary.

Martha Collins had gone into great detail reminding Mary how she and Mary's father had warned her that he was a no good spoiled rich man's son who would treat her like a possession instead of a marriage partner.

She was not surprised to learn that he had hit her. It continued saying that when Mary decided to quit hiding out at the women's shelter where she was undoubtedly hanging around with the trailer trash whores that were always there, she could come home to Pennsylvania. Martha had her room prepared for her.

She had always kept it ready because she was certain that the marriage would end. Mary should have listened to them and never made such a foolish mistake.

No wonder Martha knew so little about Mary's life in Burlington. She had pushed her away and belittled her in her time of need instead of helping and supporting her.

Below her mother's letters, Jack found a few from some of her old college girl friends filled with chatter about their lives. There was nothing to indicate that Mary had confided in any of them about the problems in her marriage.

At the bottom of the papers, Jack came across what he had been hoping for. It was a Valentine card. Inside was a note that read.

...To my super sexy tutor. You make it hard for me to succeed with my studies, because it would mean that I would be able to spend less time with you. I hope you like your present and always think of me as time passes us by.

Wow, Jack thought, here's a real smoking gun. It's too bad that it wasn't signed so he could identify the shooter.

He put the papers back into the box after he had dumped out the other items onto his table.

Jack sorted through assorted framed pictures from her wedding day, a folded up caricature of her in a bikini, probably done by a Church Street artist, a little pink drink umbrella and a women's Rolex watch.

Jack got the Valentine back out and re-read the message inside... Always think of me as time passes us by... he wondered if this watch could have been the gift that had come with the card?

Jack decided that he would ask Gary Robbins about the watch and card when he returned Mary's box. It could be something or nothing depending on what Robbins knew about it.

Jack knew that people, especially those whose lives were dictated by schedules like teachers, always wore their watches. Why hadn't this one disappeared with Mary? Was it the gift from the ardent student?

Rolex's were not back up watches left in drawers or boxes. They were too expensive. She would have taken off to sleep and bathe, but not otherwise. Time would tell.

Jack called Eddie Michaels at the marina and told him he would be staying out overnight, but would be back at first light in the morning to open up for the day. Eddie should not come into work until noontime.

He knew that he needed some cocooning time to plot out how he should proceed with his quest. A night alone on the lake was a good setting for that. He went below to the cabin, turned on the CD player, loaded his favorite Barry Manilow, Neil Diamond, and Barbara Streisand discs, and settled in with his notes and thoughts so he could sort them out and plot his course

CHAPTER 44

Jack was up before dawn on Tuesday morning. First light arrived at 5:40 A.M. He pulled up anchor and headed back to Marble Island Marina.

He tied up his boat in its slip at 6:30. He took his time with his morning routine, as he would be on duty at least until noon when he had told Eddie Michaels to come in.

When he had finished his daily routine, he retired to his desk in the marina office. Pouring a cup of coffee from the pot he had made, he began to review the plan of action that he had worked out the previous night.

Firstly, he would chase down the current residence of Michael Meyers. He was still the top suspect on the short list. The super sexy tutor note in the Valentine card closely resembled his comment in the yearbook.

Secondly, he needed to find the co-editors of the 1978 year book. One of them might have knowledge that would lead to a heretofore unknown person of interest. He would start there and see what evolved.

If nothing came up from those inquiries, he would have to pursue Conrad's relationship with Mary. Jack knew that doing this would be dicey. The O'Brien family name carried a lot of sway. He hoped that it would be unnecessary to turn over that rock.

Jack started with an internet google search for Michael Meyers. Eleven pages popped up with his initial entry.

Michael Meyers was apparently a famous name. Most of the references led to a movie actor's fan club web page. He entered "Burlington Vermont" and it narrowed the search down to four references, all from newspaper stories.

The first was an old Free Press sports section article reporting that Michael Meyers, senior forward, had been thrown off from the Burlington High School basketball team as the result of attacking an opposing player during a game against Rice High School in December 1977.

The next was another article from the Free Press. It reported that Michael Meyers, age 20, a Burlington construction worker, had been arrested for DUI after a high speed chase in 1980.

He had wrecked his car while attempting to elude the police, and had ended up having to be physically restrained when he tried to run away on foot after knocking down an officer at the accident scene.

The third reported that Michael Meyers, age 21, Burlington construction worker, had plea bargained charges from DUI, attempting to elude, and assault on a police officer, down to careless and negligent driving, accident resulting, in January 1981.

The breathalyzer test that was performed at the accident scene had been done before Meyers had received his Miranda rights, so it was thrown out by the court. The Chittenden County District Attorney had worked out the deal for a guilty plea to the lesser charge.

Jack remembered that the case had become a campaign issue in the Chittenden County District Attorney's reelection campaign the following year.

His opponent had claimed that his office was incompetent and used it as an example to underscore the allegation. The District Attorney had lost the election.

The final newspaper article, dated July 1982, was attributed to the Glens Falls New York Daily Gazette. It reported that Michael Meyers age 23, a construction worker from Burlington Vermont, had been arrested the previous September for the brutal abduction and rape of a 25 year old elementary school teacher.

She had been left for dead in the woods. He had been tried and was found guilty and had been sentenced to 25 years to life in prison. He was to serve out his sentence at Attica, a maximum-security prison located in western New York.

An appeal was planned on Meyer's behalf by the public defender. There was no further report of an appeal on the internet. Meyers and his attorney must have failed in their attempt.

Jack decided he would be taking a road trip out to Attica. It was near Buffalo in the western tip of New York State. He needed to arrange a few days off to accomplish this. It would have to be delayed until after July 4th.

He googled the names of the year book co-editors next. The first, Susan Ames, got no hits. Jack figured that she might have gotten married and he would find out her new surname from her co-editor Jamie Griggs.

His name showed up as an Essex Junction land surveyor. He was listed in the phone book yellow pages. Jack wrote down his telephone number on his legal pad and turned off the computer.

A phone call to him resulted in talking to an answering machine. He left his name and a message for Griggs to call back and hung up. Jack figured it was a one-man operation and Jamie was out in the field. It was time to play the waiting game again.

Jack returned his notes to his boat. Then he called his sister Carol.

He asked her to call his other siblings and invite them to the fireworks celebration. It was taking the easy way out, but he was not up for rejection just now. He forgot to tell her about seeing Kelly Cosgrove the previous evening.

He was walking back to the office when a truck and boat transport trailer from Allen's Marina pulled into the storage yard. Jack walked up to meet the driver. He was there to pick up Paquette's boat.

The note said that he was moving it to the North Hero location because he had been dissatisfied with the facilities at Marble Island. Jack said that there were no yard fees due. He offered his help in loading the boat and trailer. The driver replied that he had it under control.

He would call the marina owner and give him a heads up on Captain Crunch. Although he did not know Doug Allen well, Jack felt that he had a personal responsibility to inform him about the character of his newest dock tenant.

At least Allen's Marina was 30 miles away to the north in the inland sea portion of the lake. That was a fair distance, and Paquette would have to deal with a drawbridge, which was in service only during limited hours of operation, and the notoriously shallow "Gut" to reach the broad lake.

He doubted he would be seeing Paquette again. The chances of his being able to successfully navigate that course at his present level of proficiency was somewhere right between slim and none.

CHAPTER 45

Thursday was June 30th. Only five days to July 4th thought Jack as he finished up his morning marina routine. He went into the office and made a note to call the ice company and the coca-cola distributor and increase his standing order for the long weekend.

It would be the busiest four days of the year at the marina. Virtually all of the boaters would have guests on board to watch the Colchester fire works on Sunday night. Many would be traveling to Burlington by water for their celebration on Monday.

Carol called to tell him that their brothers Tom, Tim and Matthew would be there in time to depart at 3:00 P.M. for the fireworks on the 4th with their spouses and kids.

Mark wasn't sure; he was hoping for another invitation, she told him. Jack thanked her. He told her that he would call Mark back to confirm. He would see her and their mother when they arrived on Monday.

Jack went back on board his boat before he called his brother Mark at his workplace. Mark was the sales manager for a local office equipment business.

When he came on the line Jack told him that he hoped, for their mother's sake, that he and his wife would attend with their teen-age son. It would make her very happy to share the evening with all of her children and grandchildren.

Please call as soon as his plans were confirmed, as their attendance would make a difference in how many extra life jackets would be needed, as well as how much food Jack needed to buy for their dinner on the lake.

He hung up without saying good-bye. It wasn't very polite, but he hadn't thought that Mark's initial response to the invitation was either. It would definitely be a while before another invitation would be extended.

Jack looked over at his refrigerator in the galley and spotted the paper that Kelly Cosgrove had given him. On impulse, he dialed her number.

He got her answering machine as he had expected. He asked if she would like to join him to watch the July 3rd fireworks in Colchester aboard his boat at the marina. Dinner would be included.

He apologized for making the invitation on a machine. He did it because he was in a conundrum he explained. He did not want to wait to contact her, but had not wanted to disturb her at her office. He looked forward to hearing back from her.

Kelly was the controller for a large non-profit agency in Burlington. She had told him that she worked from 6:00 A.M until 5:00 P.M. each weekday.

Work and her 13 year old cat named Buffy was her life, she had told him during their conversation on Monday evening. It had sounded eerily similar to what his own life had become, except for the cat.

Sharing an evening with her after 35 years would be a wonderful experience for him he thought. Jack hoped that she would accept his invitation. It could be the start of a rekindling of their old love.

It would be nice to share a bit of his life with her, even if it only led to their becoming friends again. He was lonely.

As he walked back up the dock to the marina office to call the suppliers on his list he remembered another of Newell Johnson's adages. ...Life goes on with or without your participation, so you need to be your own advocate... popped into Jack's mind.

Thanks dad he thought, now how about a little help to show me the patience to deal with my brother.

CHAPTER 46

A few boaters started to show up to provision for the long weekend early on Thursday afternoon. They were the cruisers who would be away from the marina until late on Monday, or even Tuesday morning. They stopped by the office on their way to their boats.

Jack asked that when marina boaters were planning to cruise overnight, they leave a rough float plan at the marina office before they left. If they became delayed significantly, they could call him and let him know.

If they were more than several hours late returning and Jack had not heard anything he would try to reach them by cell phone.

If that failed, he would notify the Coast Guard. Part of his morning routine was to take inventory and determine if anyone's boat was AWOL.

One time two years before, this practice had allowed a stolen yacht to be recovered by authorities before it could disappear from the lake and on to a transport trailer operated by an out of state stolen boat operation.

The last thing Jack wanted was for someone to be broken down and adrift on Lake Champlain. Storms could come up unexpectedly and with extreme severity. Part of the promise that Malletts Bay Marina made to their boaters was to help insure their safety while using their facilities.

Jack had interpreted that this commitment extended to their safety while out on the lake as well as on the docks. After all, the lake was the largest part of their facilities, wasn't it? Newell Johnson certainly would have thought so.

Jack had Eddie Michaels stationed in the parking lot so he could direct the boaters who would be staying on board their boats to park in the storage yard after he helped them load up the garden way carts with their supplies.

Jack manned the docks, helping to transfer supplies to boats, and returning the carts to the parking lot. He also took care of any fuel customers. The afternoon turned to evening before it was slow enough to send Eddie home and close things down for the night.

A call came in on his cell phone as Jack was locking up the fuel pumps. His caller ID showed J&S Griggs. He walked to his boat and notes while answering. He said hello Jamie, thanks for returning my call.

A woman responded that she wasn't Jamie. She was his wife Sue. Jamie was out of town for a few days. Could she help out with anything in the meanwhile. She handled his work schedule for him.

Jack explained that he was calling seeking information about the Burlington High School class of 1978. Sue said that she and Jamie were both alumni of that class.

On a hunch, Jack asked her if her maiden name was Ames. She replied that it had been. He got two yearbook editors for the price of one.

He gave her the cover story he had been using about Mary Robbins disappearance and asked Sue if she remembered her. She said that she certainly did. Ms. Robbins had been one of her favorite teachers. She had been in both her junior and senior English classes.

Did she remember any rumors about her having an affair with another teacher or student? Ms. Robbins had been especially close to the kids she had tutored. There had been some gossip about a couple. She had thought it nothing more than school kid's imaginations.

Did she remember which of the kids the gossip had been about? One had been a jock named Michael Meyers. Lots of muscle and looks with not much in the brains department.

The other was a rich kid named Conrad O'Brien whose twin brother Louis had recently been elected Mayor of Burlington. She did not really know either of them; they had not hung out in the same circles in high school.

Jack did not correct her about Conrad and Louis's relationship. It was not necessary, and he knew that it might put her off to be corrected by him.

Was there anything else that she could recall regarding either of the boys?

After Michael Meyers had been thrown off the basketball team, his demeanor had changed in the classroom. He started to cut up all the time and became a distraction to the rest of the class.

Ms. Robbins had thrown him out of class in April. He had bragged to everyone that it was because she had asked him to fool around when she was tutoring him and he had turned her down.

What about Conrad? When he was a junior, he never seemed to be engaged in learning. He had been too busy trying to seduce as many female students as possible. Once he had had sex with one, he would move on to the next. He was a real Casanova, or had thought so anyway.

He had seemed to mature during his senior year. About halfway through he had really buckled down and worked hard. It had changed her impression of him. He became more like his brother.

Jack thanked her for helping. He asked that she talk to Jamie and see if he thought of anything to add to her observances. If he did, Jack would appreciate a call from him.

When he hung up Jack knew that his trip to Attica to see Michael Meyers could be a very interesting, if Meyers would meet with him and chose to cooperate.

Jack got one more call on Thursday night. It was from Kelly Cosgrove. She would enjoy very much having dinner and watching the Colchester fireworks display with him. She was familiar with the location of the marina, and would see him on Sunday afternoon at 2:30.

CHAPTER 47

Friday and Saturday were even busier at the marina than the previous few years had been. Jack and the staff were kept running, refilling the vending machines and pumping fuel for boaters. All of the transient dock spaces were filled, as were the guest moorings. The time flew by.

Eddie Michaels would cover for Jack at the marina on Sunday evening so he could entertain his guest. He called his sister to let her know that Mark would not be with them on Monday. He had never called back.

Carol said that she would make up a suitable excuse for Myrtle to minimize her disappointment.

He told her about his date with Kelly, she cautioned him to go slowly. This was the first time he had seen another woman since his divorce and he should not push too hard on the rebound. Jack laughed and reminded her that his separation from Sally had occurred seven years ago, and his divorce had been finalized for 5 ½ years. There was no rebound he responded.

He was just taking another step on the path that was the rest of his life. Be happy for him, not worried about him. Jack had to promise to call her Sunday night after the fireworks and fill her in on the details before she would hang up.

Sunday morning was quieter. A lot of boaters had spent Saturday night on board at the docks partying, and were sleeping off a little excessive drinking.

It gave Jack an opportunity to wash down the bathrooms, restock the toilet paper and paper towel dispensers, and enjoy several cups of coffee.

He had spent the previous evening cleaning his boat, a chore that he performed too seldom. He wanted everything to look shipshape when Kelly came on board.

He was surprised that he was so anxious to make a good impression on her. They had known each other for 39 years after all. This was just two old friends getting together to catch up.

At 2:15 P.M. Kelly walked down to the marina office. Jack was just finishing going over things with Eddie. He had forgotten that she had always liked to arrive a few minutes early.

When he introduced Kelly, Eddie asked if she had a brother David. He told her that they had graduated from high school together the previous year.

Kelly laughed and thanked him for the compliment. She told him that David was her nephew. He was 34 years her junior. Eddie told her that she did not look anywhere near that old. Jack commented that he agreed and told Eddie good-bye.

He walked down the dock with Kelly and helped her board his boat. He showed her around, instructed her on the operation of the marine head, and went back on deck to cast off while she was changing into her bathing suit.

He steered out of the marina and set a course for Little Reef. It surrounded a small island referred to as Beer Can Island because fishermen liked to anchor there, fish for bass, and drink beer. In the old days, they had thrown their empties in the lake.

The bass would not show up on the reef for another two months when the water was cooler. The anchor would set well in the sand on the bottom, and it would be a nice spot, away from the crowds that would congregate in the inner bay. Jack thought it would be a great location to watch the fireworks from, and allow them some privacy.

Kelly came on deck. She looked terrific. Jack found himself at a loss for something to say. She had changed so little, and he so much, that he simply did not know how to start a conversation with her.

Kelly came to the rescue. "Jack, this is one of my father's favorite spots to go bass fishing. We spend many a Saturday morning out here in September and October.

Bass fishing has become one of my favorite distractions. When I was a kid I spent a lot of time fishing for perch with a neighbor. Then I got away from it when I became a teenager."

"After my divorce I started to go out for bass with my dad and Uncle Bill. The only rules dad has are that I have to bait my own hook, clean my own fish, and tell my own lies."

He laughed and they started to swap fish stories. The awkwardness disappeared and they settled in on the upper deck of the boat. For the rest of the day they enjoyed each other's company.

After the fireworks were over, while they were waiting for the boat traffic from the inner bay to thin out, Jack turned up his CD player, playing the Temptations greatest hits, and they danced on the foredeck.

Jack lit up a cigar as he was motoring back to the marina. The time was 10:30 P.M. It was the perfect way to end a perfect day. They tied off the boat and he walked Kelly back to her car.

She told him that the next time they got together, she would cook dinner for him. He told her he hoped that it would be soon and they kissed goodnight.

He watched her drive away from the marina and walked back to his boat, calling his sister as he walked down the dock. She asked him how things had gone and he told her they had gone great.

Carol then asked if Kelly was spending the night. He laughed and said not tonight, maybe next time. He went to bed wondering when the next time would be. He was really new at this… What was old is new again… was his last thought as he fell asleep.

CHAPTER 48

Monday morning Jack was up early. He finished his marina routine before 7:00 A.M. He was going to be working alone until 2:00 P.M. when Eddie and the other dock boy were coming in to take the evening shift.

There was a note saying that the ice machine had acted up the previous evening. Eddie had called the vendor's answering service.

A service technician called the office phone at 7:30 A.M. and told Jack that he would be there in about 45 minutes. He had a back up ice machine on his truck and would swap it out with the one at the marina.

Jack started to pull out the bags of ice and put them into the large chest freezer that they had in the boat shed to store extra ice to refill the machine on weekends. He was just finishing when the tech arrived.

Jack used the forklift to move the old machine out to the parking lot, and bring the replacement back to the front of the office. It would have to sit for four hours before it could be plugged in.

Jack would have to supply the needs of the boaters and collect the money manually for the remainder of the morning. It would limit his range of activity, as he could not stray too far from the office.

He decided to update his action plan on the investigation and retrieved his notes from the boat. At the top of his list was the trip to Attica Prison. Michael Meyers was where he visualized the next dots to be connected were.

He would talk to Eddie Michaels and Conrad and arrange to be gone Wednesday and Thursday. They were usually slow days at the marina. It should not be a problem.

If nothing developed from his visit with Meyers, he would have to explore Conrad's involvement some more. If Conrad also turned out to be a dead end, Jack could see no more links.

He reviewed what he had done and felt that the two steps he had planned would be the end of his investigation. He could see nowhere else to take it.

… All good things must come to an end… It did not seem like quite the right saying but Jack could not remember Newell having provided a better one.

One way or another he would soon be placing his last piece in the puzzle. Would it be completed when he put it place?

CHAPTER 49

Jack left for Attica a little before 5:00 A.M. on Wednesday morning. The drive would take about six hours and Jack wanted to arrive for the start of visiting hours at 11:00 A.M.

He had called ahead to the warden's office, explaining his reason for wanting to see Meyers. The warden's secretary had called back saying that Meyers had agreed to meet with him.

Jack arrived at 10:45 A.M and went through the mandatory strip search before he was escorted to a visitor area. It had several tables with chairs and six visible closed circuit TV cameras that he could count.

At 11:14 A.M., a prisoner was brought into the room in handcuffs and leg irons. He appeared to be about 60 years old. He was led to Jack's table and told to sit down.

Jack started his interview. "Are you Michael Meyers, age 45, from Burlington Vermont?"

Meyers answer was a simple "yes."

"Did you graduate from Burlington High School in 1978?"

"Yes" again. This was going well.

Jack decided to jump in with both feet. "What do you remember about an English teacher named Mary Robbins?"

This answer was more animated.

Meyers replied "She was my senior English teacher, until she tossed me out of her class a few months before graduation. She was also my tutor for my junior year, and the first half of my senior year."

Without prodding, he continued "She was a real sexy looking lady and she used it on the kids in school. I came on to her several times but she always blew me off. It wouldn't have bothered me except I knew that she was screwing one of the other kids in my class."

"All I wanted was a little piece of the action that she was passing out with her homework."

"I was mad as hell when she threw me out of class, so I started spreading around rumors about her being an easy lay."

"I made up a story about how she came on to me, and I blew her off. That was what I told anyone who would listen was the reason that she had tossed me out of her class."

"My old man had to come to school for a meeting with her in the principal's office. I had to apologize to her for spreading the rumors."

"That was the only way the school would allow me to finish my senior English requirement with another teacher. I never talked to the arrogant bitch again. She was nothing but a tease, and probably some guy did her in when she wouldn't put out after putting on the tease to him."

It was a surprisingly frank statement, Jack thought. He had just a few more questions for Meyers.

"Did you kill, or do you know who might have killed Mary Robbins?"

" No, I didn't and no, I don't."

"What was the name of the kid that he knew she was screwing?"

"His name is Conrad O'Brien."

"How do you know that Mary Robbins and Conrad O'Brien were screwing? Did you see them together? If so when and where was it?"

Meyers replied "I had an assignment that I needed to turn in to Robbins in December 1977. My academic eligibility to play on the basketball team was in jeopardy and if she did not receive it and sign off, then I would not be allowed to suit up and play in the big game against Rice that night."

"I knew that she was at O'Brien's house tutoring him so I drove over and parked on the street. When she came out, O'Brien walked her to her car. They stood real close and talked for several minutes before he went back inside."

"That's when I got out of my car and walked over to hers to give her the paper and get her signature on the eligibility release form."

"After she had signed off on my eligibility, I asked her how long she had been screwing Conrad. She turned beet red and fumbled with her speech for a minute before she denied it."

"I could tell that she was lying. I got enough tail in my day to be able to tell when a bitch was in heat, and she was panting."

Jack told Meyers "Your suspicion is no proof that anything had been going on between Conrad and Mary Robbins. If that's all you've got then you've got nothing. Without real tangible evidence, all that your story amounts to is a fairy tale."

"Are you still trying to get even with Robbins for tossing you out of class? It sounds like you're just blowing smoke to deflect suspicion from yourself."

"Did you lose your temper and kill her? Where did you dump her body? Do you have an alibi for May 26, 1978?"

"The woman you raped and beat in New York appears to share many of the same character traits as Mary Robbins. Were you reliving what you had done to Robbins and got caught before you could kill her and dump her body?"

Meyers replied "As a matter of fact I do have an airtight alibi for the day that Robbins went missing. I skipped my exam that day and went to Boston for a Red Sox game with my old man."

"They were playing the Yankees at Fenway. It was the only pro baseball game I ever attended. My old man wrote a note for me to take to school the next day saying I was sick at home."

"They even allowed me to take a makeup exam the following Monday after school. It was the only time I ever played hooky with my old man's permission. If you want to check with him, he'll back me up. I even kept the ticket stubs as a souvenir. They're still in my bureau drawer at my old man's apartment in Burlington."

"Besides, I didn't rape or beat up the bitch in Glens Falls. I screwed her, when I picked her up at a bar. She was there with her boyfriend and they had had a fight. We did it right in the parking lot behind the bar."

"Her boyfriend stormed out and I moved in on her. She was drunk as hell. It was easy. Afterword I left her there and drove back to the motel I was staying in."

"The next morning the cops showed up and arrested me. She was a convincing witness. I got the shaft. They never even looked for anyone else. I still pay the price for that lousy piece of tail every day."

Twenty-five years inside was like fifty out in the free world. Meyers ended the interview with "Put that in your pipe and smoke it, Jack Ass Johnson."

He motioned to the guard and stood up to leave the table.

Jack decided not to thank him. He thought even Newell Johnson would have forgiven his lack of good manners. It was going to be a long ride home. He would need all of the time to figure out how to follow his dots to Conrad.

CHAPTER 50

He arrived back in Burlington at 7:30 P.M. His return was 24 hours earlier than anyone had expected. He had decided to drive straight through and stay at his sister's condominium overnight.

When he had called her, Carol had told him to come over and crash in her guest room. Their mother had returned to Rutland that morning.

She had asked what was going on, but Jack wasn't ready to confide in anyone about what he was going to do.

He had been busy on his cell phone during the trip home. He had called Meyer's father and confirmed his alibi first. Alec Meyers had backed up Michael's story.

The trip to the ball game had been his early graduation present to Michael. It had been the only time they had ever done anything like that together.

His next call had been to Gary Robbins. He asked Robbins about the Valentine card and watch in Mary's box. Gary said he had never bothered to open the card and read it. He had not seen it in the box.

She had received many Valentine cards from her students each year. She had thrown them all out after reading them, but had apparently missed that one.

The Rolex watch had been a birthday present to her from Gary the first year of their marriage. He had not found it in the back of a kitchen drawer until a couple of years after she had disappeared.

He had already sent all of her jewelry to her parents in Pennsylvania, so he tossed it in the box and forgotten about it. She had stopped wearing it the February before her disappearance.

She had gotten a new Seiko. When he had asked her about it she told him that she had given herself a Valentines present, since he had not bothered to get her anything.

She had said that she hated looking at the Rolex because every time she did it had reminded her that he had given it to her, and their marriage had turned out to be such a waste of time.

She had told him that she had thrown the Rolex away. He shouldn't admit it, even now, but when she had said that to him he had wanted to kill her.

The plan that Jack had developed after his phone conversations started with a call to Frank O'Brien at his home Thursday morning at 6:00 A.M. Without tipping his hand, he asked Frank to arrange for Jack and Conrad to meet at his office sometime during the day.

He told Frank only that it would be in Conrad's best interest if he had legal representation present for the meeting. The meeting was set up for 1:00 P.M. Frank assured him that Conrad would attend.

Jack went to his boat and picked up the photos that Bennie had taken. He took Mary Robbins' ledger and the Valentine card out of the Robbins' box.

He arranged his notes and prepared his evidence. He did not have anything that was tangible proof, but when he connected all the dots, it made a strong circumstantial argument that Conrad held the key to Mary Robbins disappearance.

The Bennie Richards accident was nothing but conjecture. He would have to be a poker player today, and hope that Conrad and Frank did not call his bluff.

He left the marina before 7:00 A.M. The last thing he needed to do was run into Conrad before the meeting.

One o'clock was show time. Jack was intentionally five minutes late. He wanted Conrad and Frank to be waiting so they could cut right to the chase. It worked.

They met in a small conference room on the second floor of the law offices. After shaking hands, Jack thanked them for meeting with him and started.

He slowly took out the photo enhancement showing the Donzi. He placed the original that Bennie had recorded the date and time on next to it.

Frank asked, "What is this about Jack?"

Conrad said, "This is about bullshit Uncle Frank. Jack has a fantasy that I know something about some old disappearance case that he could never solve."

Next Jack placed the Valentine card and note on the table. Conrad started to look a little concerned.

Finally, Jack pulled his notes out and started speaking. "Let's start with the Valentine card Conrad. There's a note inside that's addressed "To my super sexy tutor." Does the penmanship look familiar to you?"

"I need to remind you that handwriting analysis is an accepted practice in a court of law."

Conrad did not even bother to read the note. He said, "I gave that card to Mary Robbins during my senior year in high school."

"Was the gift mentioned in the note a Seiko watch?"

Conrad asked, "How did you find that out?"

"We can get to that later."

"How long were you and Mary Robbins having an affair?"

"That's nothing more than a slanderous lie."

"I have a statement from another of Mary Robbins tutees that says otherwise."

This was his first bluff; he knew Meyers' allegation was only speculation from a convicted felon.

Frank and Conrad held a quick whispered conversation before Conrad admitted, yes, we were having an affair. That doesn't mean I had anything to do with her death."

Jack moved the enhancement showing the Donzi over in front of Conrad.

He turned over the original so that Bennie Richards note was visible. He referred to his notes and continued.

There were three eyewitnesses who saw Mary Robbins on the path to Shelburne Point beach on the day she disappeared."

"One of the eyewitness's saw your car going into Shelburne Shipyard at the same time. You just admitted that you were having an affair with Mary."

"No one ever saw her again after your car arrived at the marina. Within a half hour of your arrival, the photo of the Donzi was taken. Was Mary Robbins the young woman in the photo with you, Conrad?"

Frank O'Brien interrupted. "Jack, I strongly suggest that if you're alleging that Conrad had something to do with Mary Robbins disappearance, that you should come right out and say so."

Jack replied, "That's exactly what I'm alleging Frank. If Conrad doesn't want to answer my questions here and now, I can go to the authorities and share what I've found out with them."

"They will undoubtedly be asking the same things in a much less comfortable environment."

Frank and Conrad decided to continue. Jack repeated his last question. Conrad answered.

He told the entire story of the day. He finished and said that he was relieved that the truth was finally revealed.

"I've been living with this secret for 27 years. I've never even been able to allow myself a close relationship with anyone since."

"What are looking for from me anyway?"

Jack had thought a lot about this moment. "Conrad, did Bennie Richards approach you for hush money because he had figured it out?"

Conrad told Jack, "That's just nuts. I barely even knew Bennie Richards' mother. I can't even remember ever meeting him. If his ghost came into this room right now and kicked me in the ass, I wouldn't know who he was." It was Jack's final bluff. It didn't work. Or maybe it did.

I'll turn myself into the authorities voluntarily, but I had nothing to do with whatever had happened to Bennie Richards. Whoever said differently was lying."

"You have no proof that I did because no such proof exists. I'll stake my life on that."

Jack's gut told him that Conrad was finally telling the truth.

Jack spent the rest of the afternoon with Conrad and Frank, discussing the best way for Conrad to turn himself in. They decided it would be best for him to go directly to the Chittenden County District Attorney, Norman Stone.

He had a reputation as a fierce litigator with a strong moral compass. It would happen tomorrow, Friday, a few minutes before 5:00 P.M. That would allow them the weekend to work out any missing details of the surrender with the District Attorney before the press got hold of it, minimizing the appearance of a preferential deal because of the family name.

Jack would not be present. It would be better if it appeared that Conrad was doing this to cleanse his conscience, bring closure to Mary Robbins family and to allow Mary's soul to rest peacefully.

Frank and Conrad agreed that the O'Brien family should pay whatever it cost to locate and recover Mary's body. Conrad would make a personal apology to Gary Robbins, Mary's parents and the Burlington community.

The O'Brien family would also underwrite the costs of the investigation, which would need to be done, in order to prove that Mary's death had indeed been an accident, and not a result of foul play.

There would be a perennial Mary Robbins Scholarship established to promote teaching as a profession. Pamela Abbot would be named to pick the annual recipients of the scholarship.

It would be made anonymously no sooner than six months after the case was closed. There would be no appearance that Conrad was trying to buy mercy for himself.

Jack finished the meeting with another saying that Newell Johnson had often reminded him of when he had been alive. He could not remember whom it was originally attributed to but it was a good thought for Conrad to go home with

…. And the truth shall set you free…

CHAPTER 51

Jack returned to Marble Island Marina feeling drained from the meeting with Conrad and Frank O'Brien. He sent Eddie Michaels home early and settled into the marina office to catch up on what he had missed over the past two days.

There was a message from Heather Cosgrove to call her. He wondered what that was about. He would wait until after he had closed things down for the night before calling her back.

The ice distributor wanted to bring back the repaired machine and get the loaner back tomorrow at 8:00 A.M. He would have to empty it early in the morning.

Doug Allen had called. Jack returned that one immediately.

Doug wanted to thank him for the heads up Jack had given him about Paquette. He had nearly run through the gas dock the previous day. Doug had the Grand Isle Sheriff's Department come out.

Paquette had blown a .016, twice the legal limit and would not be endangering anyone on the lake for at least a year.

Because Doug had warned his dock crew to keep an eye on Paquette, the attendant at the gas dock was watching closely and had been able to jump out of the way before the collision.

Paquette had taken off out on the lake after the collision, not realizing that he had put a hole in the hull of his boat under the waterline. His boat had sunk.

When the police boat caught up with him, he was swimming in 60 feet of water. The dock fees he had paid in advance would just about cover the damage.

The jerk had canceled his insurance policy the day after he moved his boat to the marina. Jack apologized for not warning Doug sooner. Doug replied not to worry about it. He appreciated having being told.

At 7:00 P.M. Jack locked up the fuel pumps and office. He went to his truck, got out the items that he had taken to the meeting at Frank O'Brien's office and trudged to his boat.

He wanted to crawl into bed and pull the covers over his head for a couple of days. Classic signs of cocooning, he thought. He decided to fight the urge, fixed a peanut butter and jelly sandwich, and took it and an Excel on deck to watch the sunset.

He finished eating and remembered the message in his pocket to call Heather Cosgrove. She answered on the second ring.

Heather had called Jack to invite him to a surprise anniversary party that she was hosting at her parents camp for them.

She had urged Kelly to extend the invitation, but Kelly had not wanted to make him feel pressured to meet the family so soon. Heather had reminded her that Jack had known the family for 40 years, so there would be no pressure.

Jack thanked her for the invitation. Before he could accept, he would call Kelly and talk to her about it. He did not want to show up at a party and make her feel uncomfortable because of his presence.

He would let Heather know through her sister whether he would be there or not. He appreciated her thinking of him. He called Kelly's number and got her machine. He did not leave a message.

Great, he thought, she's probably out with someone. He should not expect that she would be hanging around waiting for her phone to ring. She had said that she would invite him to dinner at her house the next time.

He should have waited for her to call him. No wonder he had never been good at dating. He did not have the skills for it.

He lit up a cigar, stared at the sunset, and beat himself up emotionally before going to bed for the night. As he was nodding off it occurred to him that he might find himself without a job, or a place to dock his home very soon.

Forcing your employer to turn himself in to the authorities for a crime was not a good way to insure one's job security… Don't put the cart before the horse… He thought, thanks dad, goodnight. And he dozed off.

CHAPTER 52

Jack worked quietly all day Friday. He took care of the ice machine in the morning. A fuel delivery truck showed up in the afternoon.

Eddie Michaels worked the evening shift, so Jack was able to watch the TV local news at 6:00 P.M. There was no report about Conrad's surrender. The timing must have been spot on.

At 7:00 P.M. Jack heard someone from the dock hailing him, asking permission to come aboard. It was Kelly Cosgrove. She had brought dinner with her.

Although he was pleased that she had felt comfortable coming by without calling first, he couldn't stop himself from joking with her a little.

He yelled abandon ship into the empty cabin. Jack had to chase her back up the deck about 30 feet and apologize for his lousy sense of humor.

Kelly gave him a playful swat on the arm and came on board. The meat loaf she had brought was delicious.

After dinner, they retired to the upper deck in the canvas chairs with coffee. Kelly asked Jack if he thought it was too soon for him to attend a family gathering, explaining that her parent's anniversary was the next weekend and there was going to be a surprise party for them.

Without telling her that Heather had already called him, Jack said that he would love to see her family again and would enjoy attending.

As Kelly was preparing to leave, Jack asked if she had ever spent a night on a boat. He quickly added that he could bunk out on the couch if she would like to stay. Kelly responded that it would not be necessary.

They went to bed together. It was as if 35 years had never passed. Although neither of them got much sleep, they were both in fantastic moods the next morning when Kelly went home at 5:30 A.M. to take care of her cat.

She would come back on Sunday afternoon to go boating. Jack told her to bring her fishing gear; they could go out on a reef and do some fishing. Kelly laughed and told him that they might not get much fishing done, but she'd bring her tackle just in case.

As Kelly drove out of the parking lot and he was walking back to the docks to perform his morning routine Jack asked himself if it was possible to still be in love with her after all the time that had passed. He knew the answer was that, at least for him it was.

At 10:00 A.M. Conrad and Frank came by. They went to the marina office where they could talk privately. Frank started the conversation.

"Jack, we want to bring you up to speed on things. Yesterday afternoon we met as planned with Norman Stone. He accepted Conrad's statement that I had prepared for him without any changes or additions.

"Stone immediately called a judge, and Conrad was quickly processed and released on personal recognizance. The media won't be informed until Monday morning."

"Conrad and I, as well as Louis have discussed how Conrad's business affairs will be handled in the likely event that he is incarcerated."

"We all agreed that you've been doing a great job with the marina, and we would like you to continue."

"If you are willing to assume a few additional responsibilities, namely watching out over the rest of the Island property, and overseeing the household budget for Conrad's fiancé while he's away, there will be an increase in your salary to compensate you for those additional responsibilities."

Jack was caught off guard by the proposal. Can I get back to you after I've thought about it for a few days?"

Conrad said, "That's not a problem Jack, as long you don't disappear in the meantime. I want no more disappearances in my life."

All three laughed at his comment. Jack thought he could feel the presence of his father, and Charles O'Brien in the office with them. He did not voice the feeling to the others.

After they shook hands ending their meeting, Conrad asked Jack to put the Donzi back in the water and run it over to Louis's camp on the other side of the island.

"I've decided to keep the boat in the family, and am giving it to Louis and Martha as an early anniversary gift. I never want to step foot on it myself again, but it should never belong to anyone other than an O'Brien. Louis and Martha will enjoy and appreciate it more than I ever would anyway."

In the early afternoon, Louis stopped by with two Ashley torpedoes'. They went to Jack's boat, sat down with a couple of beers, and lit their cigars.

Louis started the conversation.

"Jack, I can't thank you enough for the discretion and consideration you have shown the O'Brien family. You could have gained a lot of attention for yourself if you had gone to the authorities instead of working with Frank and Conrad to minimize the collateral damages that would have occurred to the rest of the family."

"Louis, you should be thanking the spirits of my father, and your Uncle Charles, not me. Had Charles not been so caring an employer to my father during the final years of his life, and so gracious and generous to my mother after his death, things might have been done differently."

"My father taught me, by his own example, that one should always show loyalty to those who have earned it. The O'Brien family earned my dad's, and mine, a long time ago."

They finished their cigars in silence.

CHAPTER 53

The initial publicity regarding Conrad O'Brien's confession and public apology died down quickly.

In early August, a salvage operation was launched from just off Juniper Island. It had taken only a few days with the help of a high tech search and recovery mini-sub for Mary Robbins remains to be recovered.

After an extensive and expensive autopsy was performed, it was determined that they were Mary Robbins remains.

It was also conclusively determined that a cast of the large rock that she had collided with from the cove matched up perfectly with the damage to her skull which had been found the cause of her death. The death was ruled accidental.

Conrad pled guilty to a variety of charges including three felonies. Failure to report an accident... death resulting, leaving the scene of an accident... death resulting, and failure to aid authorities in an official investigation.

The judge came down with a harsh sentence. Five to fifteen years in prison and a $100,000 fine. Conrad would be eligible for early release on account of good behavior in 2 ½ years.

The entire episode from Conrad's confession to his sentencing was completed by the first week in September.

Jack had kept out of sight during the trial. Initially following the confession, he had answered many questions asked by the States Attorney. The meetings were held quietly, after normal hours at Jacks insistence.

He had remained busy both at Marble Island and in his renewed relationship with Kelly Cosgrove. He had almost been able to put Benny Richards' death out of his mind. He had followed his gut, done his best, and come up empty.

When Gary Robbins came by the marina and handed Jack the reward for solving Mary's disappearance and death, a certified check for $50,000, he knew what he was going to do with the check immediately.

He called Jean Richards at the mini-mart and asked if he could stop by and drop off the box with Bennie's things in it. She said that of course he could.

He retrieved the box from his boat, put the check in his wallet, and drove down to Burlington. When he got to the mini-mart Jean and Terry were both there.

He placed the box on the cashier's counter in front of Terry and started to pull out his wallet to give Jean the check.

Terry looked in the box and pulled out the picture that had been so instrumental in solving Mary Robbins murder. She pointed to it and asked Jean if she knew where they went?

Jack was shocked into silence. After a minute, he asked Terry what she was referring to.

Terry responded that she had found Bennie looking at the old photos one night and spotted the magnetic signs on the tow truck. She told him that they would look neat hanging over the cash register at the store.

Bennie did not know where they were and had written a note on the back of the photo to remind himself to ask Jean about them.

Bennie had his accident a few weeks later, and Terry had forgotten about the signs until just now when she saw the photo again. Did Jean know where they were?

What a bombshell! Jack recovered and pulled out the check to give to Jean. He told her that the case would not have been solved if not for Bennie's picture.

Jean handed the check back to Jack. She said it was ridiculous to think that Bennie had in any way known about Conrad O'Brien and Mary Robbins. The only person who deserved the reward was Jack Johnson. She was just proud to know him.

She knew that he had done his best to determine if Bennie's death was an accident or not. Jean would never be able to thank him enough for all of the trouble he had gone through to help. She knew that his father would have been proud.

While Jean and Jack were talking, Terry was going through the box again. She asked Jack why there were empty cigarette packs in it. Jack told her that he had taken them out of the van before it had been disposed of.

John Patch

She said that Bennie never smoked. It had bothered him constantly that his mother did. He had been certain that his father's heart attack had been caused by his smoking, and had sworn that he would never indulge in such a harmful bad habit. He had made Terry make the same promise.

It was okay to sell them to others who could poison themselves if they so chose, Bennie had said.

He was in business to supply what his customers wanted to buy, not to question their judgment. There was no way that he ever would have had empty cigarette packs in the van.

Then she asked about the soda can. Bennie never allowed anyone to have open beverages in the van. The coffee cup he used was spill proof. That was the only beverage container she had ever seen him allow in it.

When they were traveling and stopped for a soda, they always had to finish them before they got back in the van and turn them back in for the five-cent refund.

If they had purchased them at a vending machine, Bennie would throw the empties in the trash. He had been a little weird about things like that.

Jack thought about Terry's acclimations for several minutes. He was starting to see a bunch of dots forming in his mind.

He asked Jean and Terry if he could borrow Bennie's box again for a little while. They told him that he could keep it.

Except for the coffee mug Terry added, she would like to keep that to use for herself.

He pulled the plastic bag with the coffee mug out of the box and left it for Terry. He had some more work to do.

If the dots were lining up as he suspected the box on the counter held all of the evidence that he would need to prove that Bennie had been murdered.

CHAPTER 54

Jack started on his renewed quest the next afternoon after working with Eddie most of the day hauling boats and placing them in their cradles in the storage yard.

Jack had made an appointment with the Chittenden County District Attorney during the morning. He had gained a lot of trust from Norman Stone because of Conrad's confession.

A secretary called him at 11:15 A.M. The boss was expecting him at 3:00 P.M. was her message. Jack was ready. He walked into Norman Stone's office that afternoon promptly at 3:00.

He quickly explained to Stone that the reason he had uncovered the information leading to Conrad's decision to turn himself in the Robbins death was because of his investigation of Benny Richard's accident.

He informed Stone that when he had approached first the state police force and then the Burlington police department immediately following Bennie's death, they had both declined to investigate any further. Even though Jack had provided them with what he felt was more than just cause to do so.

That being said, Jack had just discovered the presence of what he felt would prove to be compelling evidence of an ongoing major crime being committed. One that Bennie Richards had stumbled across before him.

The person who was behind the crime must have found out that Bennie knew about him. Jack was certain that this evidence would prove who had killed Bennie Richards and was behind the ongoing major crime that was not yet discovered by the authorities.

Jack stated that the way to get to the person behind the crime was to first identify him as a murderer.

Because all of the evidence had been uncovered first by Bennie Richards and then by Jack, it was not as a result of any official investigation.

It was not uncovered in a police investigation and its authenticity could easily be brought into doubt. It could and would be challenged in any trial.

The result of that challenge would undoubtedly mean that not only this evidence, but also any additional evidence that was uncovered during an official investigation would be thrown out of court. The defense attorney's referred to it as fruit of a poisoned tree.

What he was proposing to Norman Stone was that he provide Jack with a little unofficial help from his office.

Jack would use his poisoned fruit to identify the criminals involved. If he could successfully accomplish this, he would call the Chittenden County crime stoppers tip line. He would anonymously report the crimes committed with the name of the perpetrator.

The tip line was overseen by the District Attorney's office, allowing them to determine if the information offered was viable, and deciding which of the local police departments should follow up on the supplied information.

Based on the tip, Stone could have his in house state police detective conduct an official investigation and uncover unimpeachable evidence for the state.

It would avoid any taint on the case that would otherwise be attached because of Jack's unofficial investigation. Jack went on to say that, he could accomplish what he needed without help from Stone.

It would greatly increase the chance that Jack, as Bennie Richards had, would be discovered and killed if he used independent resources to process the evidence that he possessed.

A few of the technicians working in independent labs were regularly offered cash incentives from outside interests for information that was advantageous for them to become aware of.

As Stone was no doubt aware, industrial and criminal espionage was quite common in the 21st century. Would he help?

Stone's immediate reply was that his office could offer Jack no help whatsoever. He needed plausible deniability to any knowledge of Jack's suspicions.

This meeting would be recorded as a short personal thank you from the Chittenden County District Attorney to a private citizen for his help in the Mary Robbins disappearance case. Jack should leave the office immediately.

Stone ended the meeting suggesting that Jack should keep his cell phone close to him and expect a call from an old friend who was still on the job.

Jack handed Stone an envelope on his way out of the office. On the front was written, open in the event of Jack Johnson's death. He told Stone it was his last will and testament.

CHAPTER 55

It was Friday night; the sun was setting at around 7:00 P.M. The marina was now closing at 5:00 P.M. because the busy boating season was coming to its end.

Kelly Cosgrove was coming and bringing dinner. They would spend the night on the boat at the docks. Jack was taking off from work early tomorrow.

They were going to go bass fishing. They planned to stay out on the reefs Saturday night so they could fish on Sunday morning before Jack went back to work at noontime relieving Eddie.

It was a clear night. Bundled up in blankets, sitting on the upper deck, they talked about their relationship. Jack ended up proposing marriage for the second time in their lives.

Kelly's response was to ask why he was in such a hurry. He said that he understood where she was coming from. He would not ask again. When she was ready, she could propose to him. He would wait patiently.

Saturday morning, Kelly's father and Uncle Bill picked her up in their boat to get out on the reefs early. Jack arranged to meet them shortly after noon at Beer Can Island. He would bring lunch for all. With a quick kiss good bye, Kelly jumped on board her father's boat and they headed out.

Jack performed the morning routine that was such a part of his life quickly. Eddie Michaels showed up at 9:00 A.M. and the boat hauling routine resumed for the remainder of the morning.

As they were putting away the equipment at 11:30, Jack's cell phone rang in his pocket. He answered without looking at his display. A familiar voice said hello.

It was Vince Talbot; he was calling Jack to share some great news with him. He had just been promoted to detective, and was going to work for Norman Stone in the Chittenden County District Attorney's office. The detective he was replacing, Ken Blais, had suddenly decided to take early retirement.

Stone had called Vince personally the previous afternoon and had interviewed him. The last question was about his feelings about the Bennie Richards accident.

Vince had some misgivings about his initial report after he and Jack had revisited the sight of the accident and had gone to Captain Leonard to express his doubts. Leonard immediately picked up the phone and called Burlington Police Chief Michael Kelly with Vince present.

It had been a short conversation that ended with Leonard saying he would take care of it into the phone. Leonard had then refused Vince's request to revise his report, saying that there was not sufficient cause to do so. The Burlington Police Department had done an investigation and found nothing out of the ordinary.

Talbot had accepted the decision at face value at the time. He had thought no more about it until Stone had brought it up during the interview.

Vince started to tell Stone about his own feelings that the case might have closed too quickly. He told Stone what had transpired when he had talked with Captain Leonard about his doubts.

He then mentioned that Jack had expressed interest in the accident. He was cut off by Stone who told Vince that he was well acquainted with Jack Johnson. If Talbot still had any doubts, he should talk to Jack about them.

Stone ended the interview telling Vince that in the unlikely event that he received the promotion he would be starting at Stone's office the following week.

Only official business would be allowed during regular business hours. He'd better plan do any snooping with Johnson on his own time.

Vince figured he had blown the interview. Three hours later Captain Leonard told him that he was should pack his desk. He was moving to the big leagues, the Chittenden County District Attorney's office.

Whom did Jack know that had pulled the strings and gotten him that promotion? There were many troopers with more seniority who had also been up for promotion and had been passed over.

So what did Jack know about his sudden promotion. Should Vince be thanking him for pulling some strings? Jack told Vince that he had absolutely no knowledge until this minute that there was anything going on regarding him at all.

He congratulated Detective Talbot; The District Attorney had obviously been impressed with his abilities during the interview. Vince should accept that Stone had chosen the best candidate for the job.

Then he told Vince that it was quite coincidental that he was calling today. It must be kismet. Jack had been reviewing the contents that he had removed from Richards' van and had discovered something among them that should not have been in the van.

He explained that Bennie had a weird rule that would not allow any open containers in the van, with the exception of his spill proof coffee mug.

If Jack met Vince and gave him an empty soda can, could he do him a favor and have it fingerprinted for him? If he could get Jack an identity from the prints, Jack could chase down the owner of them and see how the soda can had ended up in the van.

Vince asked Jack if there was something going on between him and Norman Stone that he needed to know about. Jack replied that Vince really did not need to worry himself about silly suppositions like that.

He and Stone were acquaintances. The District Attorney would never conspire with a used up old fart like him.

Jack was just asking a favor from Vince as a friend. Stone need not and indeed should not be bothered with any details.

Johnson was simply trying to fulfill a promise he had made to Jean Richards to investigate Bennie's accident. Would Talbot help him do that?

Vince agreed to help, ending the conversation with the statement that he already been told by his new boss that it would be acceptable to help Jack Johnson as long as it was on his own time.

It certainly seemed a bit contrived to him. Jack accused him of being an overly suspicious detective, adding that it was a good trait for someone in his new position to possess.

Jack suggested that they meet for lunch on Monday. Vince said that would be fine, that his lunch hour was noon to 1:00 P.M.

They decided that Jack would pick him up outside Stone's office and they would go to Breakers. Jack would be buying.

Jack was only a few minutes late arriving at Beer Can Island. He dropped anchor just off the reef near to the Cosgrove boat.

His lunch guests motored over and tied off on the starboard side of the boat. Kelly opened the cooler that the bass they had caught were in. There were several beauties inside.

She gleefully exclaimed that she had out fished both her uncle and father. Her father added that she would certainly show Jack up as well. They all laughed and had lunch.

After they ate lunch, Dave and Bill Cosgrove left in their boat for a different spot. Jack and Kelly settled in on the stern of the boat enjoying the afternoon. They caught several keepers, and threw back a dozen smaller ones.

Jack cooked cheeseburgers and potatoes for dinner. It was followed by a fabulous sunset that ended the day. Kelly and Jack slept soundly, rose early, and got in several hours of fishing on Sunday morning before returning to the marina at noon.

Kelly stayed with Jack at the marina for the afternoon. They talked about the fact that their parents would be leaving for Florida in several more weeks.

Dave and Karen, Kelly's parents, had a winter place south of Tampa. Myrtle would be returning to her modest home in Naples. Kelly commented that they were not getting any younger. Jack replied that neither were they.

Kelly then asked Jack if he had plans for Monday evening. He told her he had not made any. She asked him if he felt like going shopping for a ring.

He said that he only planned to buy two rings for her, one for their engagement, and the second for their marriage. Kelly replied that had thought a lot about it since last night. It was time for Jack to buy the first one.

CHAPTER 56

Monday at noon Jack picked up Vince Talbot for lunch at Breakers as planned. Afterword Jack drove Vince back to the District Attorney's office.

They pulled into the public parking garage where Talbot's car was parked. There had been no discussion over lunch of the Richards accident. Jack had not wanted to take the risk of being overheard.

The conversation at the restaurant had been limited to talk about mutual acquaintances from their days on the Burlington Police Department.

Jack pulled out the sealed plastic bag containing the soda can and handed it to Talbot. Vince asked him how he could be so certain that the owner's fingerprints would be in the system.

Jack admitted that he could not be sure, but he had a very strong feeling in his gut, and his gut was seldom wrong.

Vince got out of the truck, telling Jack that he would get in touch in a couple of days, after he had time to have the prints processed. He hoped Jack's gut was in good working order.

Jack returned to the marina. He and Eddie Michaels were able to finish hauling all of the boats that had been left over the previous weekend to be put away for the season.

The docks were empty looking with only fifteen boats left in the water. There would be more showing up throughout the week as boaters who summered elsewhere dropped their boats off for winter storage at the marina. They would be busy again next Monday.

Jack cleaned up quickly and drove to Kelly's house in Essex Jct. to pick her up for their shopping trip, and dinner out. It was seldom that Jack would eat two meals at restaurants on the same day, but they had decided to do their shopping first, and then grab a quick supper at Al's French Fries on their way back to Essex Jct.

Jack had been ambushed. He realized it immediately when they started shopping. Kelly had previously been looking at engagement rings and had already picked out the one that they were going to purchase for her. He could tell from the way she looked at it in the cases at the first jewelry store that they visited.

Rather than take several hours looking elsewhere before returning to purchase the pre-chosen Blue Sapphire and Diamond one that she wanted, Jack exclaimed that it was precisely what he had pictured for Kelly.

She quickly agreed with his excellent taste and they left the store with it. The ring had coincidentally been the right size for her left ring finger.

They shared a quick supper at Al's, and went back to Kelly's house. Jack went into the house with Kelly and they watched an episode of The Soprano's on HBO.

He had only a set of rabbit ears antenna hooked up to the television set on board his boat, so Jack had never seen the show before. He was less than impressed by its content.

Kelly said that it was a show that grew on you, like Sex in the City did. Jack doubted either of those shows would grow on him.

He left after it was over and drove home hoping to fall asleep quickly. The bed felt empty without Kelly sharing it with him. He thought about his father and his fiancé.

When Jack and Kelly had broken up in 1970, Newell Johnson had tried to console Jack. It was the only time Jack could remember that his dad had not been able to offer any advise, idiom, or saying that addressed the pain that he had been in from a broken heart.

Newell had finally stated that he had never experienced what his son was going through. The only woman he had ever dated was Myrtle.

He had wished he could do something to take away the pain but did not know what that would be. He hugged Jack and then sat and cried with him.

Newell had liked Kelly and would be pleased that they had gotten back together. Just before Jack fell asleep one of

Newell's old piece of advice came to him... If at first you don't succeed, try, try again.

Did it relate to his renewed investigation into Bennie Richards' death, or his and Kelly's decision to marry, or both, or neither? Time would answer the question.

CHAPTER 57

Tuesday was Eddie's day off. Jack was working solo all day. The other dock boy had returned to college just before Labor Day. The daily routine took only about 30 minutes because of the decrease in activities at the marina during the late season.

Jack needed to collate the boater lease agreements and get them sent out to the boaters. A few always decided not to renew. When he knew how many vacancies to expect the following season, he could start to work filling them.

A waiting list with twenty names was in a file cabinet drawer. It would be referred to, top name first, until all slips were filled.

Occasionally an exception would be made and someone not on the list would jump to the top. People who purchased home sites like Dr. Rick and Paula Tomassi had, would receive a slip immediately.

Sometimes that meant temporally using one of the transient slips for a resident boater. As soon as another regular slip became available, the boat was moved into it and the transient slip would revert to a daily rental for cruisers.

Jack prepared the one hundred eight lease agreements, writing in the lessee's name on the front page, dating and signing the back page as marina manager. He then placed each in large manila envelope and put the envelopes in a box.

When he finished, he hung a sign on the office door that said that he would be back in 15 minutes. He drove to the post office, paid for the postage on the boater lease agreements and drove back.

He got back at 12:45, figuring he would make himself a quick sandwich on his boat and return to the marina office. He had company waiting when he got back that would change his plans.

Vince Talbot was leaning against the marina office wall smoking a cigarette. Jack said hello. He asked Vince if he would like a sandwich.

Vince declined saying he needed to get back to work quickly. He had come out to tell Jack that he had the results of the fingerprint search.

He had used an old buddy in the Burlington Police Department lab to transfer and process the prints. He had dropped them off to him yesterday afternoon after his first day at his new job.

His buddy had called him late last night and told him to stop by in the morning to pick up the report and evidence.

When they met at the Burlington Department lab this morning, the soda can and report had disappeared.

Fortunately, there was a copy of the report on his friend's computer, as he had not dumped his trash bin file before leaving work the previous evening. His terminal was password protected.

When Vince left the lab with the copy of the report tucked under his jacket, he had felt strangely like he was being observed by someone.

Because of this feeling, he had snuck out side door and gone through a back alley when he had left the office to come to the marina. He had even borrowed an assistant District Attorney's car that had been parked on the next block.

He wanted to get the identity to Jack without letting whomever it was who was watching know about his involvement.

Now he had to sneak back in so that he could be seen leaving the building to take a late lunch. He quickly added that he did not see anything in the suspect's record that would indicate that he was a murderer.

The only things there were several old speeding tickets, trespassing, resisting arrest, spousal abuse, from early this summer and a fresh Boating under the Influence, accident resulting, and fleeing the scene. Those last charges were still pending.

Jack asked Vince if the suspects name was Kenneth Paquette. Vince asked why he had bothered with the soda can and finger prints if he had already known who he was? Jack walked up to the borrowed car with him and told Vince that he had not.

The record Talbot had provided on Paquette did not show that he had ever been charged with any serious criminal activities. The presence of a soda can with his fingerprints in Ritchie's van indicated otherwise.

It didn't take a Rocket Scientist to know that surveillance of the suspect would be the next step. Jack studied the record again, this time to learn some personal information.

From what he could glean from the file, Paquette was an independent truck driver. His driver's license included a CDL endorsement and had since the early 1990's when it was first required by law.

He was 61 years old. He lived in an expensive neighborhood in Shelburne. He drove a 2005 GMC Sierra ¾ ton pickup truck that Jack had seen. It had the diesel engine, SLE package, and aftermarket oversize alloy wheels and tires. It had to have cost close to $45,000.

His wife drove a 2004 Mercedes SUV that cost about $50,000. His 34-foot Wellcraft boat had been $175,000 the previous year. The Peterbuilt that was registered to Paquette trucking was brand new. It went for $200,000 if it was dressed up.

It looked to Jack like unless the Paquette's had inherited a couple of million dollars, hit the lottery, or was engaging in some dishonest activities of some sort, that they were living way above their means.

Jack knew that the average independent truck driver made less than $80,000 a year after expenses. A loan on the boat and big rig alone would eat most of that up.

He wrote down the address of Paquette Trucking. It was located on Kellogg Road on the Essex Jct. town line. He realized that he had passed it hundreds of times without noticing on his way to the pharmacy that serviced his prescriptions for his heart disease.

He was scheduled to take tomorrow off. He would pack some sandwiches, fill his thermos with coffee. The surveillance would start after dark tonight. He would stake out the garage and determine what Paquette was hauling, and for whom. He was quite certain he already knew.

He called Kelly and told her that something had come up and he would not be able to make it for dinner Tuesday evening. She asked Jack what had come up. He replied that it had to do with the job.

CHAPTER 58

Paquette showed up at 2:00 A.M. on Wednesday morning immediately entering his office. Jack had been waiting in his Ranger.

He was parked across the road in a warehouse parking lot where he had an open view of his trucking company's garage.

After about fifteen minutes in the office, Paquette came back out and opened the overhead door where his rig was parked. He started it up and pulled out, backing up to a 56 foot enclosed trailer that was parked next to the building.

He hooked up the trailer and pulled out. He was headed toward Route 15 in Essex. The garage was located on the Colchester/Essex Jct. town line on Kellogg Road.

When they reached Route 15 Paquette turned left and headed north, away from Interstate 89. Jack had figured that he would be headed the other way.

Jack dropped back, he would be more visible on the lesser traveled road. Paquette continued through the five corners in Essex Jct. and up the hill toward the Northeast Kingdom.

Paquette drove at just under the speed limit. Several times Jack had dropped back quite far staying barely in sight.

On one occasion when the truck ahead went over the crest of a hill, Jack turned off his fog lights and sped up to close the gap between the vehicles. He had no way of telling if Paquette had been warned about the running of his fingerprints.

If he had, he would be very wary. Jack did not want to be spotted. It would curtail Paquette's activities.

Just outside of Underhill, the third town they had slowed down for since pulling out of Essex Jct. Paquette turned onto a dirt road.

Jack killed his lights before reaching the corner. He paused at the intersection. Paquette was backing into a farmyard a few hundred yards down the road.

Jack pulled his Ranger across the road into a turnaround that was there and quickly walked the 200 yards to the farmhouse.

The truck was backed up to the barn. The lights on the truck were turned off. He slowly crept up the side yard, staying in the shadows. When he had moved beyond the front of the barn halfway down the side, he crept up to a window and peered in.

The activity on the other side of the window was no surprise to him. Paquette was busy unloading cases of cigarettes from the trailer and stacking them into the barn. The space inside that Jack could see was about two thirds full.

Suddenly a dog started barking. He was tied up near the large barn door. Jack could just make him out lunging on his chain.

Paquette put down the boxes he was carrying and walked to the dog. He released him. Jack was holding his breath.

The barking got louder immediately. Then it started to move in the opposite direction. After a minute, it was replaced by a loud cry from the large mongrel.

He ran back to the barn whimpering as he went. A minute later the odor drifted over to Jack. The dog had chased a skunk and gotten sprayed.

Paquette was screaming at the dog to get the hell out of the barn. Jack heard him chasing it toward the farmhouse on the side opposite from where Jack was crouched.

He heard the dog cry again. He decided that Paquette must have hit or kicked it. One of the two was a mongrel and the other is a dumb mutt he thought.

It seemed like a good time for him to fade away back into the shadows and make his was back to his pick up. What he had seen in the barn had confirmed his suspicions.

A little old-fashioned police work was needed now. Jack would go back to the boat and grab a few hours of sleep before undertaking it.

Things were going to be busy for the next day or two. He needed to finish things up before anyone became aware of his interest.

That could create an embarrassment for Jack and some very serious repercussions for the District Attorney's office.

He returned to the Underhill Town Offices at 9:30 in the morning. After some basic instructions from the town clerk, he opened up the property tax record files. The farm and barn were located on Yandow Lane.

Jack wrote down the owner of record and closed up the file. Once again, he was not surprised. Now he had two more dots to connect. He would then be ready to call the tip line.

He drove to Shelburne Road and went into Starbucks. Wearing sunglasses and a hat he went to the counter, ordered a black small dark roast.

While it was brewing, he asked the young woman with the Erica nametag how long she had been working there. She said since it had opened the previous year. She always worked the 6 A.M. to 2:30 P.M. shift.

He wondered if she remembered her regular customers. She said that she found that it easy to do. Then he asked her one more question as he was taking his coffee from her.

Showing a picture to the young woman, he asked her if she recognized the person in the photo. She certainly did she replied. The jerk had backed into her car in the parking lot a few months earlier. She would never forget his face.

Jack told her that someone from the District Attorney's office would be in touch and walked out. He hoped she would not remember his face as well as she had the one in the picture he had shown her. She probably would not.

He had never been to that Starbucks before, and he had not run into her car a few months earlier and taken off with her yelling at him as Kenneth Paquette had.

Jack, on a hunch, had checked the police blotter reports from the week of Ritchie's accident. The one in the South Burlington weekly paper had shown a hit and run accident in the parking lot at Starbucks that had occurred at 6:35 A.M. the day of Bennie Richards' accident.

He had thought how he would have killed Bennie if it had been his job to set it up. The easiest place to have caught him off guard was in the parking lot at Starbucks. Jean had told Jack that he followed the same routine every week.

Jack had called a Sergeant at the South Burlington Police Department that had been on the Burlington force with him years before to inquire about the officer's accident report of the incident at Starbucks.

He had found out that the vehicle that had taken off was a GMC Sierra, or a Chevrolet Silverado pick up, Silver in color, license plate unknown.

The description of the driver had matched Paquette to a tee. He had been dropped off by a woman in an expensive Mercedes SUV, also silver in color. It had undoubtedly been his wife.

When Erica James, the Starbucks employee who had recognized the photo had arrived at work a few minutes before 6:00 A.M that morning, she had noticed both Paquette vehicles parked over near the employee parking spaces in the back of the lot.

At 6:35 A.M., she was running after a customer that had forgotten their sunglasses on the counter to return them. The SUV almost ran her down as it was pulling into the parking lot again.

She watched as it pulled up next to the truck and the man had gotten out of the driver's side of the SUV. A woman exited the passenger side of the SUV, walked around to the driver's side, and entered and drove off.

The man had unlocked the pickup, started it, backed out of the space it had been parked in, smashed into the trunk of her car, which was parked behind it, and took off with his tires squealing.

She could not make out the license plate because it had been so dirty. The rest of the truck was very clean.

She had gotten a long look at the driver and called the police immediately. It took them about an hour before they showed up. The pickup was long gone.

The reason that it had taken the South Burlington Police so long to respond was that they were assisting with traffic control on Interstate 89. There had been a fatal accident.

Jack was driving back to Malletts bay when he placed a call to Vince Talbot's cell, knowing that he should be out of the office at lunch and the conversation would not be overheard. Vince answered right away.

Jack asked Vince to contact the State Police Records Department and ask them to fax him a copy of the prints on file from a closed case. It had been in the late 1960's. It was from the theft of the cigarette tax stamp machine.

Vince needed to compare the prints found in the warehouse to Paquette's prints. If they matched, he should call Jack immediately. He needed the answer yesterday. Don't put anything in writing, just a phone call. Make it tonight if humanly possible.

Speed was of the essence. Thanking him without waiting for an answer, Jack hung up the phone. It would be just a few more hours to show time.

Vince called back at 6:45 P.M. Jack was waiting by the phone. Vince confirmed that Paquette's prints matched some of the ones from the tax stamp theft. Jack told him to forget everything that he had done for him over the past few days.

He should expect a phone call from his boss later that evening. He thanked Vince for all of his help. He assured there would be no repercussions and hung up.

CHAPTER 59

His next call was to the Crime Stopper Tip Line. He placed it from a pay phone in Bayside Park a few miles down the road from the marina. He wanted nothing leading back to him to be found.

The message he left was that he wanted to tip off the District Attorney that a prominent local businessman named George Andrews was in possession of a stolen tax stamp machine and several hundred cases of cigarettes that had been stamped with it. He gave the address of the farm and barn in Underhill.

He also was responsible for the death of Bennie Richards Jack continued. He had hired Kenneth Paquette to kill Richards and make it appear to have been an accident.

If they showed a picture of Paquette to Erica James, who worked at Starbucks she would confirm that he had been there twice the morning of Benway's death.

The first was a few minutes before Richards stopped for coffee. The second was a few minutes after his death. Erica would also confirm that Bennie had been there and bought a coffee at about 6:10 A.M. He hung up.

Two weeks later the Norman Stone's secretary called and asked Jack if he could attend a private meeting in the District Attorney's office that afternoon.

Jack looked up at the sky, saw some dark rain clouds headed toward Malletts Bay from the broad lake, and agreed to meet in two hours at 4:00 P.M.

He and Eddie finished with the boat that was hanging from the slings and put away the yard transporter. Jack left Eddie to close up, took a quick shower and drove downtown.

Waiting with Norman Stone in his office was Vince Talbot. After greetings and handshakes, Stone sat down at his desk, flipped through the file in front of him, and opened a locked drawer on the right hand side of his desk.

He pulled out the envelope that Jack had given him and opened it. Taking out the paper inside he read the name written on it and handed it to Vince Talbot who read it also.

Stone broke the silence asking Jack how in hell he had known that George Andrews was distributing cigarettes with counterfeit tax stamps on them. How had he figured out that he was responsible for Bennie Richards' death? Jack replied with two words... his gut...

Stone then asked Vince to bring Jack up to speed regarding the investigation and its findings. Vince quickly ran down what had occurred. Paquette had, as it turned out, been handling special shipping projects for Andrews for many years.

After a little hard questioning; intertwined with bits of evidence, and a good bluff, Paquette had become very cooperative, especially when it was explained to him that his cooperation would be taken under consideration when the time came for sentencing him for murder. That time would definitely arrive sooner not later, he was told.

The critical mistake that Paquette had made was backing into another car in the parking lot at Starbucks when he picked up his truck leaving the scene of the accident.

He had been seen by Erica James, the owner of the damaged car. She had a good description of him and his truck but had been unable to get the license plate number as it had been all muddied over.

When Vince had followed through on the anonymous tip that came into crime stoppers at Stone's request, and shown Paquette's picture to Erica James she recognized him immediately. She had told him about Paquette having been there twice the morning that he had hit her car.

As Vince had been primary investigating officer at the scene of Ritchie's fatality, and had talked with Jack about his questions regarding the particulars of the accident, he had pieced together how things might have gone down.

They had picked Paquette picked up immediately. When he realized that he had been caught dead to rights, and the promise of a good word from Norman Stone was dangled in front of him, he sang like Barry Manilow.

Paquette admitted that he had killed Bennie Richards with a blow to the back of his head. He had used a baseball bat to deliver the blow. He had snuck into Bennie's van when he had stopped at Starbucks for coffee, killed him right in the parking lot, driven him to the spot at the Winooski Bridge, placed him in the driver's seat, and put the van in drive so it went over the embankment.

He said that his wife had picked him up and driven him back down to Shelburne Road to get his pickup truck. The entire thing had only taken ½ hour from start to finish.

Not only did he finger George Andrews as the man who paid him to kill Richards, he also informed them of all of the illegal cigarettes he had transported for him over the years.

When they compared his prints to the ones found in the stolen truck found in Boston way back in the 1960's they matched.

Paquette also admitted that he had stolen the tax stamp machine with Andrews and transported it to Boston in the stolen truck.

He had gotten an emergency call from George to pick it up and bring it back to the barn in Underhill Vermont just before the operation in Boston had been busted in the early 1970's. George had received a tip about the raid.

Both George Andrews and Kenneth Paquette were currently being held without bail in the maximum-security wing at the Chittenden County Correctional Center.

When Andrews was arrested, his son-in-law Bob Brendon had contacted Stones office and offered to turn state's evidence against George in exchange for amnesty. Stone listened to what he was offering and accepted the terms.

Brendon had inside knowledge about several other criminal enterprises. He also had tapes of George and Burlington

Police Chief Michael Kelly discussing the payments for information that Andrews had been paying to Kelly's offshore bank account.

George had always used Brendon's office phone for conversations with Kelly, and Brendon had decided to take out an insurance policy in case his father-in-law and he suffered a falling out. Chief Kelly would be retiring very soon, without his pension.

The meeting finished with Stone reminding Jack that officially, he and Vince knew nothing of any involvement that Jack had been involved with regarding this entire case.

Unofficially they had both wanted to thank him for his help. Without it, George Andrews, Kenneth Paquette and Chief Michael Kelly would never have been caught.

CHAPTER 60

Jack woke up on December 1st next to his wife Kelly and step-cat Buffy in their brand new queen size bed. His brother Tom and sister-in-law Helen had moved to Florida permanently with their dogs and sold their home in South Hero.

Jack had been facing moving back with his sister Carol for the winter. It would have been okay but she had started a serious relationship with a man she had met at a Burlington Elks Club dinner at a Labor Day celebration dinner. Two's company three's a crowd they say.

He and Kelly were definitely still in love, or in love again, depending on which of them you asked. They decided that as they were both getting older, not to mention their parents, that they should get married without a long engagement.

Just before Myrtle Johnson and Dave and Karen Cosgrove had returned south for the winter season, Jack and Kelly got married at a small family gathering held at the Cosgrove camp, located in Malletts Bay, of course. They took a short honeymoon trip to Maine.

On November 1st, Jack hauled his houseboat and placed it in the storage yard. It was the last boat hauled at the marina, and would be the first one launched the following spring.

The marina was closed down for the winter. Real estate sales were tapering off. Conrad's fiancé was on an extended vacation visiting friends in California. There was little at Marble Island to look after.

Louis O'Brien IV had announced in mid-November the formation of an exploratory committee to look into a possible run for the United States Senate when Senator Joseph Leddy had announced that he would be retiring at the end of his term. They had shared the podium at a joint press conference for the announcements.

Jean Richards and Terry Richards had filed a wrongful death civil suit against George Andrews just before Thanksgiving. The amount they were seeking was $2,000,000. Jack hoped they would win.

Chief Michael Kelly on the 28th of November had been indicted by a Grand Jury of accepting illegal bribes in exchange for secret police information. He had resigned immediately.

The Burlington City Council and the Burlington Police Commission stripped him of his pension in an emergency joint meeting that very night.

Jack Johnson was trying to decide what he could do to be a productive member of his new family during the winter months. He had it narrowed down to either taking a job at The Home Depot in Williston, or trying to write a book, or maybe both.